'It is funny, it is perceptive, it deals with major concerns —illness, aging, death, the encroachment of big government. But Pym handles them so exquisitely, with such love and humanity, that we chuckle our way through, and only later recognize that she has a message for all of us.'
—*Miami Herald*

'She surprises comedy and sadness from the most banal and cozy moments without ever managing to be dull.'
—*The New York Times Book Review*

'*A Few Green Leaves* is a beautifully written, very delicate comedy.'   —*Times Literary Supplement* [London]

'[It] is like a musical coda. . . . It will please new readers and old alike. . . . Her direct, sharply ironic style is almost like speech overheard—the voice of a writer who has come to terms with life and who has no illusions about it. . . . A few green leaves are all anyone needs.'
—*Baltimore Sun*

'Readers . . . will find it exact, gently amusing and (except for that dubious happy ending) genteel-ly heartbreaking.'
—*Kirkus Reviews*

'Barbara Pym's best achievement, though, with *A Few Green Leaves* is that it reminds us with some ladylike determination that there'll always be an England of wise spinsters and country retreats, part of the backbone of a bulldog nation known for its inability to admit defeat.'
—*Houston Post*

A FEW
GREEN LEAVES

A FEW GREEN LEAVES

Barbara Pym

A PLUME BOOK

PLUME
Published by the Penguin Group
Penguin Books USA Inc., 375 Hudson Street,
New York, New York 10014, U.S.A.
Penguin Books Ltd, 27 Wrights Lane,
London W8 5TZ, England
Penguin Books Australia Ltd, Ringwood,
Victoria, Australia
Penguin Books Canada Ltd, 10 Alcorn Avenue,
Toronto, Ontario, Canada, M4V 3B2
Penguin Books (N.Z.) Ltd, 182–190 Wairau Road,
Auckland 10, New Zealand

Penguin Books Ltd, Registered Offices:
Harmondsworth, Middlesex, England

Published by Plume, an imprint of New American Library,
a division of Penguin Books USA Inc. Previously published in an
Obelisk/Dutton Paperback edition.

First Plume Printing, November, 1991
10 9 8 7 6 5 4 3 2 1

 REGISTERED TRADEMARK—MARCA REGISTRADA

Printed in the United States of America

A FEW
GREEN LEAVES

1

On the Sunday after Easter – Low Sunday, Emma believed it was called – the villagers were permitted to walk in the park and woods surrounding the manor. She had not been sure whether to come on the walk or not. It was her first weekend in the village, and she had been planning to observe the inhabitants in the time-honoured manner from behind the shadow of her curtains. But seeing the party assembling outside the pub, wearing tweeds and sensible shoes and some carrying walking-sticks, she had been unable to resist the temptation of joining in.

This annual walk was a right dating from the seventeenth century, Tom Dagnall, the rector, had told her. He was a tall man, austerely good-looking, but his brown eyes lacked the dog-like qualities so often associated with that colour. As a widower he tended not to attach himself to single women, but Emma was the daughter of his old friend Beatrix Howick and rather the type that the women's magazines used to make a feature of 'improving', though this thought had not occurred to Tom. He saw her only as a sensible person in her thirties, dark-haired, thin and possibly capable of talking intelligently about local history, his great interest and passion. Besides, she had recently come to live in her mother's cottage and he felt he had a certain duty, as rector, to make her welcome.

'The villagers still have the right to collect firewood – "faggots", as the ancient edict has it – but they're less enthusiastic about that now,' he said.

'Most of them have central heating anyway or would rather switch on an electric fire when they're cold,' said the rector's sister Daphne. She was fifty-five, some years older than her brother, with a weatherbeaten complexion and white bushy hair. She spoke with feeling, for the rectory was without central heating, but this was not the only reason why her annual Greek holiday was the high spot of her life. She now joined Emma and her brother and began asking Emma whether she had settled down well in the village and whether she was going to like living there; impossible questions to answer or even speculate on, Emma felt.

Behind them walked Martin Shrubsole, a fair, teddy-bear-like young man with a kindly expression, the junior doctor in the practice headed by old Dr Gellibrand – Dr G. as he was called – who was rather past such things as walking in the woods though he would often recommend it to his patients. Martin's wife Avice walked a few paces in front of him – a characteristic of their married life, some thought. She had been a social worker and was still active in village do-gooding, a tall, handsome young woman, now beating down the encroaching weeds on the footpath with a stout cudgel.

'This path is supposed to be kept *open*,' she said fiercely. 'Soon the nettles will be growing over it.'

2

'You can use nettles for all *kinds* of things,' said Miss Olive Lee, one of the long-established village residents who remembered the old days at the big house, as she never tired of reminding people, when the de Tankerville family had lived there and Miss Vereker had been governess to the girls. Since then the house had changed hands several times, and as the present owner made little impact on village life it was natural that interest should be concentrated on the past.

'Nettles? Yes, I'm sure you can,' said Emma, turning politely to her. She had not yet spoken to Miss Lee, only heard her singing in church, her voice hooting and swooping like an owl or some other nocturnal bird. 'Would they be something like spinach when cooked? I must try them some time,' she added doubtfully, wondering how far living in the country need go. 'Oh, is that the house?' She stopped walking to stand and gaze at the grey stone mansion now coming into view. Staring up at its blank windows she longed for some intimate detail to manifest itself, even if it were only some small domestic note like a scrap of washing hanging out somewhere. But the windows were as unwelcoming as closed eyes.

'Sir Miles is not in residence,' Tom explained. 'He usually avoids the weekend of the annual walk. In any case, he's more interested in his shooting.'

'He avoids *us*?' Emma asked, puzzled.

'Well, not us specifically, but I expect there'll be a crowd of villagers – they'll be coming along too.'

At that moment a figure did appear on the terrace, but it was only Mr Swaine, the agent, looking quite genial when he identified the approaching party, such eminently respectable people sponsored by the rector

3

and one of the doctors, not at all the sort to come farther than they were permitted or to take any kind of liberty.

'A nice day for the walk,' Tom called out.

'That's what comes of having a late Easter,' said the agent, as if giving Tom the credit for it, perhaps even thinking that it was in his power to fix the date of the festival.

'Your daffodils are lovely this year,' said Miss Lee, giving the agent credit for Nature.

'Yes, we do rather pride ourselves on those,' he agreed.

Emma glanced at the flowers in the distance. She was becoming rather tired of daffodils. Their Wordsworthian exuberance had been overdone, she felt, crammed into cottage gardens and now such poetic drifts of them in the park and woods. She would have liked to have seen the woods bare in winter, the stark outlines of noble trees – but the rector's sister had broken in on her thoughts.

'One goes on living in the hope of seeing another spring,' Daphne said with a rush of emotion. 'And isn't that a patch of violets?' She pointed to a twist of purple on the ground, no rare spring flower or even the humblest violet but the discarded wrapping of a chocolate bar, as Tom was quick to point out.

'Oh, but soon there'll be bluebells in these woods – another reason for surviving the winter,' she went on. The braying of a donkey at dawn that morning had taken her back to Delphi and the patter of delicate hooves on stone, and she walked on dreaming of the Meteora, the Peloponnese and remote Greek islands as yet unidentified.

At her enthusiastic outburst young Dr Shrubsole moved away from her, hoping that she had not noticed his withdrawal. Although he was a kind man and keenly interested in the elderly and those in late middle age, his interest was detached and clinical. He enjoyed taking blood pressures – even felt an urge to pursue the group of elderly ladies round the rector with his sphygmometer – but was disinclined to enter into other aspects of their lives. He felt that the drugs prescribed to control high blood pressure should also damp down emotional excesses and those fires of youth that could still – regrettably – burn in the dried-up hearts of those approaching old age. Daphne's outburst about living to see another spring had disturbed him and had the effect of making him join his wife in systematically beating down the undergrowth with his stick, as if violent action could somehow keep Daphne under control.

'This *is* supposed to be a public footpath,' Avice repeated. 'And what's that untidy heap of stones?'

'It *might* be the site of the D.M.V. – deserted medieval village,' Tom explained. 'It's somewhere here, as far as we know.'

Emma reflected on the cosiness of the term D.M.V., which reminded her of a meat substitute she had once bought at the supermarket when she had been trying to economise, T.V.P. was it? She smiled but did not reveal her frivolous thought.

'And all this dog's mercury,' said Miss Lee, 'surely that ought to be controlled?'

'Yes, I'm sorry about that,' said Tom, as if he could somehow have prevented its growth, 'but of course it *is* a sign of ancient habitation, dog's mercury.'

The party digested this information in silence. They

had now moved some distance away from the house and were walking past what looked like a ruined cottage in the woods. Yet, apart from its somewhat overgrown surroundings, it did seem as if it could be lived in, Emma felt. There was a romantic air about it which had been lacking in the house. She began to speculate on its possible history. 'Perhaps some of these people would know,' she said innocently, as the sound of a transistor radio heralded the approach of a party of villagers.

Tom laughed. 'I doubt it,' he said, but he felt glad, rejoiced almost, that they were exercising their right to enter the park and woods very much as they must have done in the seventeenth century, except for the mindless mumbling of the radio which its owner had not troubled to turn down. He said as much to Emma and she agreed that it was good to see the old right still maintained, though she reflected that the radio was not the only difference between now and three hundred years ago. It was noticeable that all the younger people were wearing jeans, but that the older members of the villagers' party were wearing newer, smarter and more brightly coloured clothes than the rector and his group.

Greetings were exchanged on an equal level. Tom made no attempt to enquire after relatives or children and grandchildren or even livestock, as the Lord of the Manor or his own predecessors might have done. He had noted among the villagers Mrs Dyer, the woman who came to clean at the rectory, and her presence inhibited any attempt at that kind of conversation. He knew that very few of them would be at Evensong. Of his own party this afternoon he could rely only on his sister, Miss Lee – and possibly Miss Grundy ('Flavia'), a

6

woman somewhat younger than Miss Lee, but still very much of uncertain age, with whom she shared a cottage, might also be there. But Tom suspected that Miss Grundy's preference was for Solemn Evensong and Benediction rather than the simpler village service which was all that he could offer. The young doctor and his wife seldom came to church and Emma, though she had been once out of curiosity, was an unknown quantity. He knew from her mother that she was some kind of scientist, and that she had come to the village to write up the results of a piece of research on something or other. It occurred to him that even if she didn't come to Evensong, she might be helpful in other ways. She might be a good typist, though he could hardly ask her to do such menial work, or even be expert at deciphering Elizabethan handwriting, a skill none of his willing lady helpers possessed.

2

After the walk Emma went back to Robin Cottage, so named by a former owner because the bird had once appeared when he was digging his vegetable patch and perched on the spade. The cottage now belonged to Emma's mother Beatrix, who was a tutor in English Literature at a women's college, specialising in the eighteenth- and nineteenth-century novel. This may have accounted for Emma's christian name, for it had seemed to Beatrix unfair to call her daughter Emily, a name associated with her grandmother's servants rather than the author of *Wuthering Heights*, so Emma had been chosen, perhaps with the hope that some of the qualities possessed by the heroine of the novel might be perpetuated. Emma had so far failed to come up to her mother's expectations but had become − goodness only knew how − an anthropologist. Nor had she married or formed any other kind of attachment. Beatrix would have liked her to marry − it seemed suitable − though she did not herself set all that much store by the status. Her own husband − Emma's father − had been killed in the war, and having, as it were, fulfilled herself as a woman Beatrix had been able to return to her academic studies with a clear conscience.

Emma, if she thought about her name at all, was reminded not of Jane Austen's heroine but rather of Thomas Hardy's first wife – a person with something unsatisfactory about her. Now she made herself a cup of tea, feeling that she might have asked the rector and his sister back to share it with her. But then she realised that she had no cake, only the remains of a rather stale loaf, and anyway *he* would have Evensong. She knew the times of the services and had been to church once but did not intend to become a regular churchgoer yet. All in good time, when she had had a chance to study the village, to 'evaluate' whatever material she was able to collect. For the moment she would go on writing up the notes she had completed before coming to the village – something to do with attitudes towards almost everything you could think of in one of the new towns. Here, in this almost idyllic setting of softly undulating landscape, mysterious woods and ancient stone buildings, she would be able to detach herself from the harsh realities of her field notes and perhaps even find inspiration for a new and different study.

Too soon, for she had done no work, Emma began to think about supper. What did people in the village eat? she wondered. Sunday evening supper would of course be lighter than the normal weekday meal, with husbands coming back from work. The shepherd's pie, concocted from the remains of the Sunday joint, would turn up as a kind of moussaka at the rectory, she felt, given Daphne's passionate interest in Greece. Others would be taking out ready-prepared meals or even joints of meat from their freezers, or would have bought supper dishes at the supermarket with tempting titles and bright attractive pictures on the cover.

Sometimes there might even be fish, for a man called round occasionally with fresh fish in the back of his van, suggesting a nobler time when fish had been eaten on Fridays by at least a respectable number of people in the larger houses. Had there even once been Roman Catholics in the village? Then there were people living alone, like herself, who would make do with a bit of cheese or open a small tin of something.

It would have to be an omelette, the kind of thing that every woman is supposed to be able to turn her hand to, but something was wrong with Emma's omelette this evening – the eggs not enough beaten, the tablespoon of water omitted, something not quite as it should be. But she was hungry and did not care enough to analyse what her mistake could have been. It was better not to be too fussy, especially if one lived alone, not like Adam Prince opposite, who travelled round doing his job as an 'inspector' for a gourmet food magazine, spending his days eating – tasting, sampling, criticising (especially criticising), weighing in the balance and all too often finding wanting. Emma's mother had told her that before his present job he had been an Anglican priest who had 'gone over to Rome', but she had not enlarged on this bald statement. He was away now, for Emma had noticed meticulous instructions to the milkman to that effect on the complicated plastic contraption outside his door which told exactly how much milk he did or did not want.

With her omelette Emma poured out a glass of red wine from a bottle already started, which had been warming by the side of the storage heater all the weekend. She was sure that Adam Prince would not have approved of *that*, but she felt relaxed and at peace as she ate and drank. It was a moment to turn on the television, to watch idly whatever happened to be going on.

It seemed to be a discussion – two men and a woman were confronting a politician from one of the new African republics, a Sandhurst-trained brigadier, his black face glowering. The argument became heated as the participants shifted uneasily on the too-low chairs and reached down to the even lower table to refresh themselves with some kind of liquid – perhaps only water – from heavy-based dark tumblers. The chairs appeared to be covered in a kind of furry material which Emma, not having a colour set, imagined to be like the pelt of a seal or an otter. She was fascinated by this and hypnotised by the complexities of the discussion which, having switched on in the middle, she was having difficulty in following. The chairman, a mild man who seemed to be in awe of the sharp-tongued woman participant, was doing his best to see that each of the men got a fair crack of the whip, as he might have put it. It was not until Emma heard him address one of them as 'Dr Pettifer' that she realised that this was Graham Pettifer, a man with whom she had once had a brief love affair. To say that he had been her 'lover' was altogether too grand a way to describe what their association had been; perhaps even 'love affair' was not strictly accurate, for there had not been all that much love about it, no more than proximity and a mild affection. But, anyway, it would have been true enough to say that she had once known Graham Pettifer 'quite well', though she had not seen him for many years. He had gone out to one of the African universities to teach something called 'social studies' and had now, presumably, come back, perhaps even to take up an appointment in this country?

He must be getting on for forty now, she calculated, and he had improved in looks, filled out or something. She drained her glass, meditating on this. Then, seeing that there was still some left in the bottle, finished it. The wine was decidedly warm, rather over-chambré, Adam Prince would have said, but it gave her comfort and boldness. Hardly realising what she was doing, or marking the distinction between fact and fiction, she put a sheet of paper into her typewriter and began to compose a letter.

'Dear Graham,' it said, 'I've just seen you in a TV discussion! What a great bringer-together of people who haven't met for ages the medium must be! I'm living here (temporarily) in my mother's cottage, so if you' — she paused, unable to remember his wife's christian name — 'are anywhere in this direction, do come and see me.' The 'you' could very well cover a wife and any number of children, she thought, picturing a large estate car driving up one day, filled with Graham Pettifer and his family. She hadn't said anything about enjoying the discussion, she realised, but surely it was enough to say that she had recognised *him*?

In bed later that night she remembered that of course his wife's name had been Claudia — she would be able to bring that out when the occasion arose. If it ever did.

3

Monday was always a busy day at the surgery, a rather stark new building next to the village hall. 'They' — the patients — had not on the whole been to church the previous day, but they atoned for this by a devout attendance at the place where they expected not so much to worship, though this did come into it for a few, as to receive advice and consolation. You might *talk* to the rector, some would admit doubtfully, but he couldn't give you a prescription. There was nothing in churchgoing to equal that triumphant moment when you came out of the surgery clutching the ritual scrap of paper.

Martin Shrubsole hurried through the waiting-room, head bent, as if he expected to receive a blow. He did not want to recognise any of the patients waiting there, preferring to be taken by surprise, but he noticed two he didn't particularly want to see — the rector's sister, and Miss Lickerish, an elderly village eccentric. Possibly they were waiting to see Dr Gellibrand, but Martin had not heard him arrive yet so it might be that he would have to see them both.

He went into the surgery, sat down, arranged himself in a receptive, consoling attitude and prepared to interview the patients. Miss Lickerish's file lay on top of the desk so it looked as if she was to be first. He pressed the buzzer and she came in.

'Good morning, Miss Lickerish.' He addressed the small bent woman in her knitted cap and ancient smelly tweed coat.

'Good morning, *doctor*....' It seemed as if she could hardly allow him his right to the title, but although he was not much over thirty he was as fully qualified as Dr G. and much more up to date in the treatments and drugs he prescribed.

'And how are you today?' he asked tentatively, for, after all, she must be over eighty and there was something about her that did not fit in with the neat rows of meek old people in the hospital where he had developed his interest in geriatrics. Still, everyone knew that people in villages were different. Those bright beady eyes had plenty of life in them and it was perfectly sensible to ask how she did.

'It's these fleas,' she said, 'and that stops me sleeping. I'd like some of those sleeping pills.'

'Well now, we must do something about that,' he said briskly. No point in telling her that he didn't just dish out sleeping tablets to anyone who asked for them. No good explaining that if you *would* take hedgehogs into your house you'd get fleas. It wasn't really the kind of problem he expected to have to face on a Monday morning when the patients were more apt to imagine themselves to be suffering from ailments they'd read about in the Sunday papers, but Martin was equal to the challenge. 'Let's get rid of those fleas first, shall we?' he said. Health visitor, district nurse, social worker, ordinary village do-gooder, even his own wife

Avice – all these could be called in to help, and a note authorising the purchase of a suitable insect powder might do the trick. 'Next, please,' he said to himself, pleased at having disposed of Miss Lickerish.

The next three patients were perfectly ordinary and, as it were, satisfactory – a youth with acne, a young married woman with a contraceptive problem, an older man needing to have his blood pressure checked. The fourth person to enter the room, smiling apologetically as if she knew in advance that she was going to waste his time, was the rector's sister Daphne.

'Good morning, Miss Dagnall,' he adopted his most cheerful manner, 'and how's the world treating you?' A silly thing to say, as he immediately realised, trotting out that old cliché. 'Sit down and let's have a chat,' he went on. The doctor needed to relax as much as the patient, even with the consciousness of a full load still slumped in the waiting-room.

Daphne was not exactly sure what, if anything, *was* the matter with her. She was depressed (or 'in a depressed situation'), she longed to get away from the village, from the damp spring of West Oxfordshire, to live in a whitewashed cottage on the shores of the Aegean.

'Do they have cottages there, as we know them?' Martin asked, playing for time. Why on earth didn't she go to Dr G.? he wondered. She must have been his patient long before he (Martin) came into the practice. He could not know that Daphne had deliberately chosen him because she knew only too well what Dr G. would say to her. ('We're all getting on a bit – it's been a long winter – very natural to feel a bit under the weather – go and buy yourself a new hat, my dear' –

15

his panacea for most feminine ills, when women hadn't worn hats for years. Such old-fashioned advice and he wouldn't even prescribe suitable tablets.) She hoped for better things from Martin Shrubsole.

'Of course I can't leave my brother,' she said. 'I suppose that's the trouble, in a way.'

'You don't like living at the rectory?' If this were so it was ironical, for the beautiful old grey stone rectory was the one house in the village that he and his wife coveted. '*That's* the house I want,' Avice had said.

'It's so big and rambling,' Daphne went on hopelessly. 'You've no idea how difficult it is to heat.'

Avice had pointed out that they hadn't even got night-storage heaters, Martin remembered, just a few paraffin stoves and rather inefficient ones at that. Would they be eligible for some additional heating allowance? he wondered. Probably not, as they were neither of them pensioners yet. Did Miss Dagnall wear warm enough clothes? Was her blouse adequate for this chilly spring day? 'Of course I could recommend woollen underwear,' he said jokingly, hoping to jolly her out of her depression.

'Don't talk to me about wool,' she said. 'You know my brother's obsession with local history — now he's discovered that in sixteen-eighty something people had to be buried in wool.'

'You've always lived with your brother?' Martin asked.

'Oh no — only since his wife died, though that's some time ago now. I made a home for him — it seemed the only thing to do, the least I could do, people said.'

'What did you do before that?'

'I had a little sort of job, nothing much, a sort of

16

dogsbody in a travel agency. I shared a flat with a woman friend.'

Perhaps she was a frustrated lesbian, Martin thought, his mind moving on somewhat conventional modern lines. Women living together in these days might suggest that, but Daphne was, of course, older. He shot a quick glance at her weatherbeaten face and untidy mane of white hair. Perhaps a new hair-do might help her — Martin was that much more up-to-date than Dr G. and his new hat — but obviously he couldn't suggest it.

'Let's take your B.P., shall we?' he said, falling back on a more conventional treatment. Her arm was thin and dried up, either from Greek sun or approaching age. 'You probably ought to put on a bit of weight,' he said. 'How's your appetite?'

Going out of the surgery, clutching her bit of paper, a prescription for *something*, at least, Daphne felt that Martin, the 'new doctor' as he was called in the village, had done her good. He had listened, he had been sympathetic and she felt decidedly better. Much better than she would have felt if she'd gone to Dr G. — *he* never even bothered to take your blood pressure.

The other surgery was a larger room, superior to the one where Martin Shrubsole officiated, but Dr Gellibrand still regretted the old days when he had seen patients in the more gracious surroundings of his own home. Now he was cheerfully confirming the pregnancy of a young village woman obviously destined to be the mother of many fine children. She was short and stocky, with massive thighs fully revealed by the unfashionably short skirt she was

17

wearing. It seemed entirely appropriate that Dr G., now in his late sixties, should deal with the young, while Martin, with his interest in geriatrics, should be responsible for the elderly. Dr G. did not much like the elderly but he loved the whole idea of life burgeoning and going on. It had been a relief to him to be able to off-load some of his older patients – a young cheerful face, and Martin certainly had that, would do them the world of good. For Dr G., although well liked and respected in the village, wasn't exactly cheerful-looking – people often said that he looked more like a clergyman than the rector did, but that wasn't surprising because he was the son of a clergyman and his younger brother was the vicar of a London parish.

When the young pregnant woman had gone there was a pause and the receptionist brought in coffee. Dr G.'s thoughts now were not so much on his patients as on the visit he had paid to his brother at the weekend. 'A change is as good as a rest' was one of his favourite sayings and he could always benefit from this himself, getting away occasionally from his bossy wife Christabel. The place where his brother was vicar was seedy and run-down, 'immigrants living in tenements', he had thought, somewhat inaccurately, but although the church was not a particularly flourishing one he had been impressed and a little envious of the 'show' his brother Harry had put on for High Mass. It reminded him of the days, getting on for fifty years ago now, when he himself had toyed with the idea of taking Holy Orders. He had pictured himself officiating at various festivals of the church, preaching splendid sermons and leading magnificent processions, but had remembered in time all the other duties that went with

18

being a parish priest, not forgetting the innumerable cups of sweet tea and biscuits, as his brother never tired of reminding him. Then, perhaps because he had been christened Luke, he had seen himself as a distinguished physician or surgeon, performing dramatically successful operations, the sort of thing that one now saw on medical television programmes imported from the U.S.A. In the end, of course, it had been general practice, the much-loved physician, the old family doctor, *Dr Finlay's Casebook* rather than the more highly coloured series....

His receptionist was at the door. Had Dr G. dozed off over his coffee? The next patient was waiting and he had not pressed his buzzer. Brisk and kindly she addressed him, 'Are you ready for the next one, Dr G.? It's Miss Grundy,' she added, as if tempting him with some choice dish.

But he knew in advance that Miss Grundy would probably be very much like his other elderly female patients, unmarried women of uncertain age, the sort of patients he was glad to hand over to Martin Shrubsole. The rector's sister appeared to have handed herself over, he thought with satisfaction.

Emma, buying a loaf from Mrs Bland at the shop, wondered what was going on in the building next to the village hall on this particular Monday.

'Why, it's the surgery — Mondays and Thursdays,' she was told.

'Are people in the village ill then?' Emma asked in her innocence.

Mrs Bland seemed nonplussed, almost indignant, at the question, so Emma did not press it. Of course people were ill, always and everywhere.

Peering through the half-open doors of the surgery, she was tempted to join in what seemed like an enjoyable occasion from which she was being excluded. But remembering her role as an anthropologist and observer – the necessity of being on the outside looking in – she crept away, meditating on what she had observed. There was obviously material for a note here.

4

'August 1678,' Tom Dagnall read in the diaries of
Anthony à Wood. 'The act for burying in woollen
commences the first of this month.'

While the idea of being buried in woollen in August
seemed decidedly stuffy, it gave one a more
comfortable feeling on this uncertain spring morning in
the chilly study looking out on to the tumbled
gravestones. Daphne had placed a paraffin heater at his
side but it gave out smell rather than warmth. How
many of his parishioners, Tom wondered, had been
buried in woollen? Not too difficult to find that out
from the dates in the registers, of course. It was the kind
of job he could put on to one of his eager helpers,
women from the next village, or even Miss Lee and
Miss Grundy, a nice little 'project'. Nowadays, of
course, it couldn't apply – one was probably buried in
some man-made fibre – Acrilan, Courtelle, Terylene or
nylon, never in plain cotton or wool. One might make a
comparison here. Then he remembered Miss Lickerish
digging a grave for a dead hedgehog and wrapping its
body in a hand-knitted woollen jumper she had bought
at a jumble sale, and at that moment his sister came into

the room with coffee, telling him that she had seen Miss
Lickerish at the surgery that morning.

Why had Daphne gone to the doctor? he wondered
idly. Ought he to have shown brotherly concern?
Better not to ask for details in case it was just a
woman's thing and a cause for mutual embarrassment.
She had not seemed ill and now appeared perfectly
well, going on about the new young doctor and how
charming he was.

'Much better than Dr G.,' she added.

'Oh, surely not *better*,' Tom protested. He was
prepared to allow the old doctor his privileged position
in the village as a kind of leader of the community
equal to or even above that of his own.

'Dr Shrubsole asked me if I'd like tranquillisers,'
Daphne said proudly.

'And what did you answer?'

'Oh, I can't possibly tell you that. Consultation
between doctor and patient is a confidential matter.
Like the confessional.'

'Of course — I'm sorry I asked.' Tom, as younger
brother, had been put in his place, and that dig about
the confessional was a reminder of the time when Tom
had wanted to introduce that kind of thing — most
unsuitably — into the village.

Daphne was a poor substitute for his wife Laura, but
they had been married such a short time, it had been
like a dream. He hardly thought about her now, was
even uncertain what colour her eyes had been. He now
realised that he ought to have married again after Laura
died, but before he could even think what he was going
to do, in his bereft and helpless state, Daphne had come
running, as it were, determined to do her duty. She had

22

tried to organise the parish, to leave him free to pursue his studies which had turned out to be no more than dabblings. He could have walked with Laura in the woods, hardly noticing or caring about the remains of the deserted medieval village, the D.M.V.... Now he was alone, with the feeling that he had blighted Daphne's life, for, although she would take her annual holiday in Greece, she would never leave him now.

'He took my blood pressure,' Daphne went on.

'Oh?' Tom was uncertain whether he ought to express concern or whether the taking of blood pressure was a matter for congratulation, for it was not Dr G.'s custom to take it.

There was a clattering sound outside the study door. Mrs Dyer, the daily woman, was indicating displeasure about something. Dyer by name and dire by nature, Tom thought, nerving himself for her entry.

Mrs Dyer came into the room. She was a grim-looking woman wearing trousers and a hat which was never removed except for the occasional social event in the village hall or – one presumed – when she went to sleep, or under the stress of some strong emotion. Tom felt that there was something subtly wrong in wearing a hat with trousers, or at least her particular type of hat, but he could not have said what it was.

'Good morning, Mrs Dyer,' he greeted her, in what he hoped was a pleasant, encouraging tone of voice. 'I've just been reading here about how people had to be buried in woollen in the old days.'

'I don't know about that,' she declared. '*I* never heard of it.'

'Well, no, it was in the seventeenth century, the *late*

seventeenth century,' Tom emended, 'Anthony à Wood has it here.'

She glanced suspiciously at the volume on Tom's desk.

'If you're ready, Mrs Dyer,' Daphne said, 'I'll help you move these things.' She resented the way Tom wasted Mrs Dyer's time, and his own too, for it *was* a waste of time, trying to get her to talk about the old days, even to set up a tape-recorder in the hope that something might emerge from her pronouncements and babblings. For quite often Mrs Dyer did pronounce and even hold forth – inaccuracies poured from her lips about the 'old days' and how things were then. But her 'old days' went back no farther than the late nineteen thirties, and that wasn't quite what Tom wanted.

'You remember we're spring-cleaning this room today, Tom,' said Daphne patiently. 'I did tell you it was to be today.'

'Oh, my goodness....' Tom felt himself becoming quite ludicrously agitated, like a comic parson or absent-minded professor in a stage farce, as he shuffled the papers on his desk, dropping several sheets in an attempt to gather them together. 'Today, is it? I must get out then.'

'Yes, I think you must – unless you want to sit with a dust-sheet over you. You could go out, couldn't you? Do a bit of visiting or something?'

'In the morning?' Tom hesitated, for visiting was difficult enough at the best of times. In the morning it would seem to be impossible, though there was less likely to be television to contend with.

'You could go and call on Miss Howick, couldn't you? She doesn't work,' said Daphne impatiently,

24

anxious to get her brother out of the room.

'She does do some kind of research,' Tom said doubtfully. 'I expect she works in the morning, writes, perhaps....'

'If you can call it work,' said Daphne scornfully. 'What about the people in Apple Tree Cottage then?' There was a note of challenge in her voice and Tom knew exactly what had put it there. The people in Apple Tree Cottage, a youngish academic couple who had recently moved there, were very much an unknown quantity. 'Bohemian'-looking, with a neglected garden, often in the pub at lunch-time, never seen in church.... Tom marshalled such facts as he knew about them and decided that perhaps a morning visit might not be a good idea.

'All right then,' he said, getting up from his desk. 'I'll go out.' He, the rector, would be seen walking in the village, strolling down the main street.

Adam Prince, the food inspector, returning from an unusually arduous tour of duty, took up the pint of milk from his doorstep. At least the milkman had got the message this time, though — a shade of displeasure crossed his face — he had not left the Jersey milk, only the 'white top', as they called it, which had less cream. Then there were one or two niggling uncertainties in his mind about the restaurants he had just visited and on which he must now write his report. That celery, cleverly disguised in a rich sauce, *had* it come out of a tin? And the mayonnaise with the first course, served in an attractive Portuguese pottery bowl, was it *really* home-made? The fillet of veal, marinaded in Pernod and served with mushrooms, almonds and pineapple in

25

a cream sauce, had been on the rich side and he was now beginning to regret having chosen it. But so often in this work one *had* no choice – it was all in the course of duty. And now what? Too late for coffee, too early for a drink – though when was it ever too early for a glass of Tio Pepe, slightly chilled? And now the rector was approaching, so Adam's thoughts turned to Madeira and possibly a piece of seed cake or a Bath Oliver biscuit. Good plain English food, apart from the drink.

'Good morning!' he called out to Tom. 'Come in and join me in a glass of Madeira.'

Tom was startled, not seeing at first who had addressed him, but he caught the words 'a glass of Madeira' and then he guessed that it must be Adam Prince who was inviting him in. There was a slight awkwardness here, Tom felt, for he could not help being conscious of the fact that Adam had once been a Church of England clergyman before his doubting of the validity of Anglican Orders had sent him over to Rome. This meant that he was sometimes apt to put forward suggestions on parish matters, what *he* might have done or would do, in a way that seemed to Tom both embarrassing and impertinent. Then, too, his knowledge and appreciation of gourmet eating seemed inappropriate and made Tom feel ill at ease. So the acceptance of Adam's invitation at this moment was not at all what he had intended when he was about to nerve himself to do some parish visiting. All the same, it was infinitely more agreeable to sit in Adam's carefully furnished 'drawing-room' with a drink at his side than to carry out his parochial duties. There was even a certain enjoyment in listening to Adam going on about the places he had just visited – the over-rich or ill-cooked dishes he had tried to eat, the wines served at the wrong temperatures he had been obliged to sample.

'Tonight,' he was saying, 'all I shall be capable of eating is a plate of *spaghetti*' – he gave it an exaggeratedly Italian pronunciation – 'perfectly *al dente*, you understand – exactly twelve and a half minutes, in my opinion – with a sprinkling of Parmesan and a knob of butter.'

'Ah, butter,' said Tom, seizing on something he had heard of. 'What kind of butter?' he was inspired to ask, for he knew that there was a great variety of butters.

'I prefer Danish for *spaghetti*, otherwise Normandy, of course.'

'And what will you drink?' Tom asked, thinking of tea-bag tea, instant coffee or West Oxfordshire water.

'It doesn't matter all that much what one drinks with *spaghetti* so I shall surprise myself. I shall go to my cellar and shut my eyes and reach out to touch a bottle and then, ah then, who knows *what* it might be!' Adam's small pale eyes, like sea-washed pebbles, gleamed, and his soft plump body seemed to swell in anticipation. 'Do you ever do that?' he asked Tom. 'Just go to your cellar and pick a bottle at random?'

'Unfortunately I have no cellar, as such,' said Tom, for naturally there were cellars at the rectory, a whole floor of them underneath the house.

Adam seemed surprised. 'But wine's so much part of the job,' he said.

'Yes, of course,' Tom agreed, though he had never seen his calling in quite that way. Nor did the idea of a full cellar at the rectory accord with the half-dozen bottles of communion wine kept in the safe in the

27

vestry. 'I'm afraid the parochial church council would have something to say if one experimented with anything but the cheapest,' he added.

'Really? In *my* day' – Adam couldn't resist some reference to his former status, with the implication that he had controlled his P.C.C. rather better than Tom did – 'we managed to sample some not unpalatable Vino Sacro – we even experimented with a *white* wine on one occasion – nothing against that, you know, as long as it's the fermented juice of the grape.'

In the Roman church, Tom recalled, there was communion in one kind – the laity did not partake of the chalice and Adam was 'laity' now. He might well look back on his Anglican days with a certain amount of regret. There was no Roman Catholic church in the village, so Adam had to drive to Mass, sitting upright in his ruby-red Renault motor-car. And at the end of the journey, that rather dreadful vernacular Mass, scant consolation for one brought up on the nineteenth-century Anglo-Catholic revival and *The Ritual Reason Why* – Tom permitted himself a faint smile. 'I must see if I can't do something about ordering a better wine,' he said.

'It shouldn't be too difficult to pull the wool over your treasurer's eyes,' said Adam.

'Yes, a splendid woman. I suppose I might do that.'

'Ladies are easily deceived on some matters,' said Adam. 'I used to find it not too difficult.'

Tom felt that he ought to leave at this point and got up to go, wondering in what way Adam Prince had deceived ladies. 'I'm supposed to be calling on the Barracloughs,' he said.

'In the morning?' Adam seemed surprised. 'You

intend to break in on the tapping of the typewriter?'

'They work in the mornings, do they? I suppose you'd know something of their habits, being so near.'

Adam looked at his watch. 'They'll be going over to the pub at twelve,' he said. 'But you may just catch them in.'

Put like that it seemed even less of a good idea to call on the Barracloughs than Tom had at first supposed. It would soon be possible to return to the rectory with the prospect of lunch. Even with the spring-cleaning Daphne would be capable of providing a 'ploughman's' or her Greek version of it – a hunk of stale bread, a few small hard black olives, the larger juicier kind being unobtainable here, and something approaching a goats'-milk cheese. No butter, of course – such a decadent refinement didn't go with an Attic luncheon.

He walked slowly past the Barracloughs' cottage. There did not appear to be any curtains in the windows of the downstairs sitting-room and a whole scene lay before him like a stage set. There was a big rough wooden table at which the Barracloughs – Robbie and Tamsin – were sitting, he with his reddish beard looking like a Victorian representation of one of the Apostles, she with dark hair frizzed out in an 'Afro' style and round metal-rimmed spectacles. She was sitting at the typewriter, hands poised over the keys, he was by her side with a notebook in his hand as if dictating what she should write. 'Male and female created He them,' Tom thought. The table was littered with papers but in one corner there was a loaf of brown bread on a board, a chunk of cheese and two bottles of beer. Perhaps the Barracloughs were not going to the pub after all, but having what the politicians sometimes

29

called 'a working lunch'. Obviously it was not the time to interrupt them. Tom walked quickly past, hoping that they had not seen him staring in.

Now he came to Emma Howick's cottage and here also he expected to hear the tapping of the typewriter, but there was silence. She must be out, Tom thought, so he did not scruple to look more fixedly in at the window than he would otherwise have done. To his dismay he found himself looking straight at Emma, involved in a confrontation with her, as he might have put it. She was standing in the middle of her sitting-room with a dish of something in her hands. Tom's first impression was of a 'shape', the blancmange of his childhood, but obviously it couldn't be that. People like Emma didn't eat that kind of thing in these days – it would be a mousse, something made with eggs and cream.

Tom smiled and waved his hand in a friendly gesture, feeling it was the best he could do, having been caught staring in. Emma, still holding the dish in her hands, could not wave back, but she smiled in what seemed a cordial way as Tom passed along the road back to the rectory.

5

Emma hoped that the dismay she felt on seeing Tom passing the window did not show in her face. She had been in the act of removing a ham mousse from the refrigerator to a less cold but still cool place when she had seen him walking by, with the look of somebody about to drop in. And who, if not the rector of a country parish, had a better right to do this?

Still holding the dish she smiled back; then, to her relief, he went on. She put the mousse on a shelf in the larder with the salads she had already made. She had no idea when Graham and Claudia Pettifer would turn up, so lunch was to be cold, with soup to start and cheese to follow. It would of course have been possible to include the rector in the party — indeed, it would have provided another man — but there would surely have been a certain awkwardness in the conversation when she had not seen Graham for so long, had never met his wife and scarcely knew the rector. Besides, his sister would be expecting him back for lunch.

The impulsive letter Emma had written to Graham, after seeing him on the box and rashly finishing the bottle of wine, had been posted, regretted and then forgotten. She hardly even remembered that she had written, and certainly not what she had said, when his answer came on a postcard – a representation of a Corot painting, greyish-green trees and a shadowy figure underneath them. 'Remember how you used to like this?' he had written. She had entirely forgotten ever having revealed such a liking – had he perhaps made a mistake and confused her with somebody else? Mistakes of this kind had been known to occur between men and women.... 'Shall be in your area Monday,' the card had continued, 'so will call in the hope of seeing you – probably late morning, depending on circumstances.' What 'circumstances'? she wondered. Probably an appointment elsewhere. No mention of his wife – he had not said 'we', but it was as well to be prepared, so she had laid three places at the table. Another thing she had remembered about the wife was that she had been a student at Beatrix's college – she must remember to ask her mother about Claudia some time.

A car was cruising slowly along the village street, with a man peering around him, then getting out and going up to Emma's cottage.

'Emma!'

'Graham....' Emma was leaning over the gate holding out her hand, but then there was the business of parking the car and she was too much occupied at first in suggesting various solutions to notice that he was alone.

'Isn't your wife with you?' she asked as they went into the cottage.

'No, I'm on my own – as you see. It seemed better, somehow.'

'Better?' There was an ominous sound about this. In

what way could it have been better? She led Graham into her sitting-room and poured two glasses of sherry. They sat down facing each other.

'Well, here's to you,' she said, with unnatural heartiness. She had nerved herself for this meeting and now felt a sense of anticlimax. 'I saw you on that discussion programme that Sunday night and just dashed off a letter. I thought if you were anywhere in the neighbourhood, passing by – people often *are* in or near Oxford, and it isn't really all that far from London – it seems to be on the way to quite a lot of places....' She felt that she was babbling on foolishly, for now that Graham was actually here – had materialised, she almost felt – it was becoming evident that it was going to be rather difficult to talk to him. Even a mention of the old days at L.S.E., which she now threw into the conversation, did not do much to lighten the atmosphere. She had never before experienced the curious awkwardness of meeting somebody you had once loved and now no longer thought about.

'Well, well,' Graham said, leaning back in his chair but hardly contributing much, and his next remark was little better. 'What made you write to me?' he asked.

'A sudden impulse,' Emma said. 'I turned on the programme in the middle, but I wasn't expecting to see you – you know how it is if you see somebody you know on the box, it gives you....'

'A special feeling?' he suggested, not without complacency.

Emma refilled his glass and added a drop to her own. They sat contemplating each other. He was still quite handsome, Emma thought, if a little fatter, and his dark hair was thick and rather longer than when she had last seen him. She, Graham thought, was even thinner than he had remembered, and he disliked bony women. Surely she had been more attractively covered in the old days? Now she was wearing a dark brown skirt of a dowdy rather than fashionable length, though he was not capable of deciding just what was wrong with it. Her tight-fitting skimpy blue jumper indicated that there was pitifully little 'bosom-wise' — he smiled to himself at the phrase — to be either revealed or concealed. She was a not particularly attractive woman in her thirties with whom he had once had a brief affair — no more than that — and she had written to him, obviously anxious for a meeting. What had possessed him to respond when it seemed that he wasn't even going to get anything to eat? For there was no sign of food or any smell of cooking.

'I thought we'd have a cold lunch — I'll just go and heat up the soup. It's laid in the kitchen — I hope you don't mind.'

'Mind! I should think not!' Graham's spirits lifted at the sight of the table in the kitchen window, the red and white check cloth, the vase of tulips, cheeses, a long French loaf and a bottle of wine. Then he noticed that the table was laid for three. Of course Emma had not realised how things were.

'When you wrote,' he began, 'I thought perhaps you might have heard, though obviously you couldn't have, unless....'

'Heard what?' Emma stood with the ladle poised over the saucepan. Twice this day she had been caught at such a domestic moment, first her confrontation with the rector through the window when she was holding the mousse, and now this.

'That Claudia and I are no longer together,' Graham said.

'No, of course I hadn't heard.' Emma was understandably confused. 'Otherwise I would never have written as I did.' If only she could remember what she *had* written, kept a carbon! But impulsive letters, the spontaneous overflow of powerful feelings, never came about like that. 'I'm so sorry,' she said, not knowing whether being sorry was at all appropriate.

Graham tore at his hunk of bread. 'You needn't be sorry,' he said. 'Perhaps it was only a matter of time, and now at least I can get on with my book. Do you mind if I tell you about it?'

Of course she didn't, or could hardly have said so even if she had. But she was gratified to observe that even in the telling of a painful story he made a good meal and congratulated her afterwards on the excellence of the ham mousse.

'Lunch not ready yet?' Tom asked, tactlessly, he realised, but it was the first thing that came into his head. No doubt the sight of the bread and cheese on the Barracloughs' table and Emma holding the 'shape' in its flowered dish had turned his thoughts in the direction of food.

'It's not a question of it being *ready*' – Daphne's tone was grim – 'when there's nothing to *get* ready. I haven't had a *moment*. Mrs Dyer left for her dinner half an hour ago, but I felt I must finish this.'

'Perhaps you shouldn't have attempted so much this morning,' Tom said. 'Going to the doctor and now spring-cleaning.' If only women wouldn't work so hard, would spare themselves a little! 'Bread and cheese

35

will suit me,' he murmured. He wondered if the Barracloughs would have shared theirs with him, but he knew better than to call on his parishioners at mealtimes.

He returned to his study and was soon absorbed in Anthony à Wood, so much so that when Daphne called him twenty minutes later he did not hear her, and that added to her irritation.

6

Not a particularly successful meeting, Emma thought, as she watched Graham Pettifer's car drive away, though he had enjoyed his lunch. On leaving he had moved towards her as if to kiss her goodbye, then apparently thought better of it and retreated. But at least it had given him the opportunity to confide in her, a sympathetic female listener, and perhaps that was to their mutual benefit.

It might have been better if I'd been a novelist, Emma thought, busily washing up the lunch. There might even have been material in his story that she could use, but a sociological survey of modern marriage, under whatever title you gave it, would find the whole affair very commonplace and predictable — the kind of thing that was happening all the time. She wondered idly whether she would ever see him again. He was not going to Africa this year so would be around in the academic world, working on this book he had mentioned. Plenty of opportunity to appear on television again, either in discussions or as an 'expert' on some aspect of the news. But this time she would not write....

After a cup of tea she went back to her desk. There

was already a page in the typewriter but she felt disinclined to go on with her work. Sitting looking out of the window, she could see people going about their business in the village and she began to wish that she had chosen a rural setting for her fieldwork rather than the arid new town with its too obvious problems and difficulties. She removed the half-finished page from the typewriter and put a new one in. 'Some Observations on the Social Patterns of a West Oxfordshire Village,' she typed. Wouldn't something on those lines be acceptable and certainly more interesting? But 'village' was wrong, somehow, too cosy — the jargon word 'community' would be more appropriate. Or, again she typed, 'The Role of Women in a West Oxfordshire Community.' Couldn't she work out something like that? Inspired by the idea, she began to consider all the inhabitants of the village, as she knew them so far, and to make notes on them.

Obviously one began with the church. *The rector — the Rev. Thomas Dagnall.* Poor Tom. 'Tom's a-cold' — *King Lear*, wasn't it? Now why should something like that come into her mind when she thought of the rector? Perhaps because he was a widower and lived with his sister? House probably much too big and cold. Sister (Daphne), eager spinster, goes on Greek holidays with woman friend.

After the church, medicine. *Dr Luke Gellibrand (Dr G.)* 'The old doctor' — 'beloved' in the village, but not very efficient. Reluctant to prescribe new drugs, or indeed any drugs at all — prefers homely remedies. Lives in large beautiful old house, on a par with the rectory, but unlike the rectory adequately heated and furnished. Everything in the best of taste — formidable wife (Christabel) – coffee mornings, select sherry parties and elaborate flower arrangements in the church (they say) – almost like a lady of the manor. Expert on freezing produce – large freezer in garage. Grown-up family living away from home.

Then the other doctor – *Martin Shrubsole and wife Avice*. Nice young man, not particularly bright, but well-meaning, kind and up-to-date – fashionable interest in 'geriatrics'. Lives in tarted-up seventeenth-century cottage with modern additions, rather too small for them (three children and Mrs S.'s mother recently come to live with them). Wife Avice former social worker, rather pushing and do-gooding, probably hankers for larger more prestigious house (possibly even the rectory).

That disposed of the doctors, but who came next – possibly *Adam Prince*, the good-food inspector and former C. of E. clergyman? Prettiest cottage in the village (though Emma had not as yet been inside, she imagined carefully chosen antiques, coffee-table books and a model kitchen).

Robbie and Tamsin Barraclough. Live in old, rather ramshackle cottage near Adam Prince – neglected garden. Both academics – often in pub. Robbie B. – tall, quite nice-looking, Scots accent. Tamsin B. – rather hippy-looking. Still just young enough to wear Laura Ashley dresses and jumble sale clothes (the kind of things Emma was just too old to wear).

Miss Lee (Olive). Lives in Yew Tree Cottage. Solid, elderly, well-established village resident of type which is said to be 'the backbone of England'. Rather well-dressed, usually wears hat. Churchgoer, does brasses and flowers but on lower scale than Christabel G.

Interested in local history – helps the rector with copying parish registers etc. Member of W.I. Nice cottage with pretty garden. Probably critical of newcomers to the village? Lives with friend, Miss Grundy.

Miss Flavia Grundy. Rumoured (Emma's mother had told her) that Miss G. had once written a romantic historical novel, but it was never spoken of. A rather sad character. London high-church goer dumped in the country, pining for incense(?). Bossed by Miss Lee.

Geoffrey Poore, church organist. Lives next door to Miss Lee and Miss Grundy. Emma knew nothing about the organist except that he was a school-master, wore his hair in a long bob and was often seen in the pub.

She began to consider the village people in general. Most of the original inhabitants now lived in the council estate on the outskirts of the village and one didn't have much contact with them. There was the pub (The Bell) and its landlord whose name Emma did not know, but she had heard that he sometimes cut the grass in the churchyard. And of course there was Mrs Dyer, who did cleaning at the rectory and one or two other houses – a sharp-tongued, not very agreeable sort of woman, who might gossip maliciously and notice 'goings on', if there were any. She had several grown-up children, notably a son Jason, who had started what passed for an 'antique' shop and who had pushed a card through Emma's door bearing the ghoulish information 'Deceased Effects Cleared.' The main point of interest about Jason Dyer was that he wore a gold earring in one ear in the form of a small crucifix.

Miss Lickerish. Emma started a new paragraph to

describe Miss Lickerish, the sort of person who was difficult to classify. She had probably been in 'good service' in her youth. Now lived in cottage, tumbledown, inhabited by livestock, heated by ancient paraffin stove (with dangerously flaring yellow flame, Daphne had told Emma – 'I've tried to tell her that the flame should be *blue*, and the wick *cleaned* sometimes ...'). Tended to be outspoken. A real 'character', perhaps, was that how she should be described?

The idea that Miss Lickerish might once have been in good service reminded Emma that she had made no mention of the gentry – the people who lived at the manor. Strictly speaking, she ought to have put them first, but who or what were the gentry now? She had never seen Sir Miles or any of his family, and barely glimpsed his agent, Mr Swaine, on the walk after Easter. *Further research needed* was the kind of note one appended to something that didn't seem to be leading anywhere. The history of the manor lay in the past, in the wall tablets and monuments in the church and in the mausoleum which had been erected in memory of the de Tankerville family some time in the last century. It shouldn't be too difficult to find out something there....

Emma took the page out of the typewriter and laid it aside. This hardly counted as 'work', she felt, this idle speculating on the people in the village. Further research seemed to be needed in a good many directions, and who knew what might come of it?

7

Every morning now, especially with the prospect of
summer, Daphne woke up thinking of how she would
one day get away from the village. She, the rector's
sister, would throw up everything and go to live on a
Greek island or in Delphi or even in one of those
towers in the Mani. Ridiculous, of course, especially the
idea of living in a tower, but on this kind of an English
summer day, with the promise of spring forgotten and
the sun hidden in grey clouds, it helped her to get
through her chores.

Today she was receiving things for a jumble sale
which was to be held on the following Saturday. People
had been invited to leave their bundles in one of the
rectory outhouses but some preferred to come up to the
house, almost as if, instead of a natural feeling of
shame, they wanted their contributions to be known
and acknowledged.

Tamsin Barraclough was the first to arrive, bringing
some old broken box-files, a collection of paperbacks
and two discarded dresses. She put them inside the
porch and crept away like somebody propitiating a
heathen god. Daphne just caught sight of her hurrying
away down the drive, her long cotton skirt dragging on

42

the gravel, her frizzy hair misted with fine rain.

Adam Prince came next. It was not regarded as a man's province to fetch or carry jumble, unless it was a particularly heavy object or something that needed to be collected in a car, but he didn't count as an ordinary man who went out to work or did a 'proper' job, as you might say. This morning he was bringing a discarded suit of such good quality that he felt attention should be drawn to it, perhaps by hanging it on a rail as was done with the better garments, and he wanted to make quite sure that the rector's sister realised this. Concealed in an anonymous bundle of old curtains and a faded plush tablecloth, there was also a pair of jeans, too tight and too youthful, definitely a 'bad buy' as the fashion writers might say. He did not want attention drawn to these and took care to place the bundle underneath another one when Daphne wasn't looking.

'So very kind,' she murmured, admiring the suit. 'We get very little in the way of men's clothing.'

Adam smiled at the word 'clothing', feeling that perhaps she had not intended to use it but had found herself slipping into the jumble sale jargon or vernacular, where the things one wore were known as clothing or garments rather than just clothes.

'Here's the doctor's wife,' said Adam on the doorstep. 'She seems to be bringing a substantial contribution.'

Avice Shrubsole was wheeling a shopping basket full of children's clothes and a few of her own, with a discarded tweed jacket of her husband's on the top. A garment belonging to the doctor might be thought to possess certain magical properties, as if a touch could heal, and Daphne was suitably grateful. But she knew

43

that Avice had really come to take another look at the rectory, to emphasise how much too big it must be for the rector and his sister, and to contrive in some way to go upstairs and even into the bedrooms, which she had never yet managed to achieve.

'Do you mind if I go to the loo?' Avice asked bluntly, preparing to mount the staircase.

'Oh, there's a cloakroom on the left of the front door,' said Daphne, preparing to thwart her. 'No need to go upstairs.'

Avice retired at the same moment as Mrs Dyer came into the room. It was her morning for doing something but she spent a good twenty minutes examining and disparaging the jumble, trying to guess who had sent what. Adam Prince's jeans evoked a shout of raucous laughter and all the children's clothes were criticised for some fault in the washing – woollens shrunken or felted, or the colours faded, obviously the wrong washing-powder used, insufficient attention paid to the television commercials – Daphne had heard it all before and made no comment, letting Mrs Dyer drone on until she finally exhausted the subject. Daphne then took some of the boxes of jumble into the drawing-room, a noble, shabbily furnished room, hardly suitable for the sorting of jumble, one might have thought, but nothing in the rectory was above parish work. There might be a good tweed skirt from Mrs G. and Daphne would not be ashamed to give 30p. for this and to wear it in the autumn. It would not occur to Mrs G. that the rector's sister might one day be seen wearing her discarded clothes, they would look so different. Christabel G. might occasionally notice that Daphne was wearing a rather better skirt than usual, might even remember that she had once had a skirt in a tweed very much like that, but no further connection would be established.

The clothes in the first box were a disappointing lot — mini, Courtelle, Acrilan and other man-made fibres, nothing ample, long or of pure wool or cotton. Daphne turned to a box of oddments — chipped cups and odd saucers suitable for cat dishes, plastic earrings, an old string of pearls with the pearliness peeling off, a tattered paperback novel whose cover portrayed the bare shoulders of a couple in bed, a bundle of knitting needles, a plastic butter-dish split at one corner, an old prayer-book with no cover and pages missing, a rusty nutmeg grater, a wrist-watch not in working order, a china animal of indeterminate sex lacking an ear, a glass ditto lacking one leg, a cracked handbag mirror, a small transistor radio, a photo-frame with a faded photograph of a person on a beach, a brooch without a pin saying 'MOTHER', an empty tin of hair lacquer, a dried-up pot of foundation cream, a red collar for a small dog or even a cat, a fork with the prongs bent, an old soap dish.... Nothing much here, the kind of things that nobody would buy except possibly a child with a few pence to spend, taking a fancy to some unlikely object. Then Daphne's attention was caught by a picture framed in passe-partout, lying at the bottom of the box. It was a coloured print of a Scottie dog, looking up appealingly at its invisible master and bearing the legend 'Thy Servant a Dog.'

Holding the picture in her hands, Daphne stood up and moved over to the window. She was back forty years to the time of her confirmation, when her friend Heather had given her a replica of this very picture. For two girls of fifteen who loved animals it had seemed to them entirely suitable as a present for the occasion, and their headmistress had wisely made no comment. Why had she no dog *now*? Daphne wondered, staring bitterly out into the rain. Tom would not have objected to a dog — wouldn't even notice — the country was obviously suitable for one. She would get a dog — why not? She would take it for walks — why had she never thought of it before? When Tom's wife died, she had come running to his aid with no thought for herself. All these years without a dog! 'Thy Servant a Dog,' she murmured softly to herself, not like cats, with their cool, appraising, insolent stares. 'Passionately fond of animals,' was how Daphne might have described herself, if anyone had asked her, and how she now began to think of herself. Animals were better than people any day. But if she did get a dog and become devoted to it, as she undoubtedly would, what would happen to it when she went to live in Greece, would she be allowed to take it with her? What were the quarantine regulations? That might be a complication — better perhaps to wait and see how her plans developed....

Should she just go up to the door and ring? Emma wondered. Or would it be all right to tap on the window, since the rector's sister was standing there looking out with a faraway expression in her eyes? Had she seen her? Was she conscious that Emma was coming round to the front door with a carrier bag full of jumble?

At that moment Daphne did see her. She put 'Thy Servant a Dog' back into the jumble box and came round to open the door.

'Ah, you're bringing jumble,' she said formally, 'won't you come in?'

Emma had not been into the rectory before, so although she had meant just to leave her bundle she could not resist the opportunity of a look inside the house.

'I was just sorting these things....' Daphne was glad to be interrupted and always enjoyed the company of another woman, aware that there was a comfortable feeling about it that the company of men did not provide, or at least the company of the kind of men she came into contact with, mostly her brother Tom and neighbouring clergy. Perhaps it was too narrow a sample to generalise about....

The two women – fifties and thirties – regarded each other warily. They had met once or twice before and chatted on the field walk, though Daphne felt that Emma was too young and too different – wasn't she some kind of scientist? – ever to become a close friend; but on this dreary morning she welcomed her.

'This is just a few things,' Emma said, revealing the contents of her carrier bag. It was embarrassing to have to display a worn skirt and a shrunken cardigan and one's old underwear, even though clean. 'I fear nobody will want to buy them,' she said apologetically.

'No,' Daphne agreed. 'The village women have such marvellous things now. They wouldn't look at cast-offs – it's we who buy them. Of course it's all to the good,' she added, feeling that she ought to say something on these lines. 'There isn't the poverty there used to be.'

Emma hoped they might get on to another subject and cast about in her mind for something else to say. She could see that the room they were in, although disfigured by the bundles of jumble and the trestle table on which Daphne was sorting them, was a beautiful one with fine mouldings on the ceiling.

'This is your drawing-room?' she asked. 'It's a lovely room.'

'Well, we don't have a drawing-room as such, but this would be it if we did. And if there's a parish function that doesn't take place in the hall we have it here. We might even have a jumble sale here.' She laughed.

There they were back at jumble again. 'What a miserable day,' Emma said, looking out at the dripping trees in the rectory drive.

'Yes, isn't it. It was so lovely when the daffodils were out and it really seemed as if…. *I* know what — how about a glass of sherry? I know Tom's got a bottle somewhere.'

This pathetic revelation of the state of the rector's drink supplies caused Emma to hesitate. Tom's 'bottle somewhere' might be sadly depleted when he next came to look for it. But Daphne insisted and Emma was bound to admit that it might improve the day. The last time she had sipped sherry with somebody sitting opposite her had been when Graham Pettifer had called to see her, she reflected, wondering why she was remembering it now in these very different circumstances. She was obviously not going to see him again and there was nothing memorable about the occasion. It was only the position of a table and two chairs and two people drinking sherry that had brought it into her mind again….

'The *new* doctor, as we call him still,' Daphne was saying, 'Martin Shrubsole' — she lingered almost lovingly on the name — ' *not* Dr G.'

'Oh, I think I should go to Dr G.,' Emma said. 'It seems the obvious thing and my mother's always said how nice he is. One does have confidence in an *older* man, somehow — luckily I'm never ill, though.'

'I find Dr Shrubsole so sympathetic,' Daphne said. 'He knew just what my trouble was. I do think it's so important in a village to have a good doctor you have confidence in — the doctor's really the most important person, isn't he?'

Emma expressed surprise. If there was no active Lord of the Manor, surely the rector was the most important person rather than the doctor?

'Well, the rector's my brother, so I suppose you can't expect me to see it that way, being an older sister. There was a rhyme we used to say when we were children, when we were playing games, and I can't help remembering that,

> Each a peach, a pear, a plum,
> Out goes old Tom....'

'Oh, a kind of eeny, meeny, miney, mo,' said Emma. 'I don't know that one.' She repeated it to herself, smiling. 'Out goes old Tom....'

'His wife died, you know,' Daphne said, as if explaining something. 'Oh, it was very sad — he never got over Laura's death, in a way. And of course *I've* had to cope, given up everything, really. I've *always* wanted to have a dog.'

Emma looked at her, again surprised. 'But surely you could have a dog? Living in the country, no problem about exercising it and all that, no pathetic face at the window of the flat when you went out to work....'

It was Daphne's turn to look surprised, her imagination unable to keep pace with Emma's. 'It wouldn't have to be shut up,' she explained. 'I can't think why I've never had one — I'm fifty-six next birthday....'

Looking at her Emma could see that the sherry, besides loosening her tongue to reveal these intimacies, had made her rather red in the face. Presumably older women shouldn't drink, she thought, or women of a certain age. But what might that age be?

'I think I shall get a dog,' Daphne said, when Tom came back to lunch.

'A dog? Whatever for?'

'Oh, you know I've *always* wanted a dog,' she burst out.

'Have you? You've never said so.'

'Oh Tom, you know how passionately fond of animals I am — always have been.

Tom considered this statement in silence, his memories going back to the pets of their childhood, rabbits and guinea pigs and, yes, there had been a dog once. But a child thrusting lettuce leaves through the bars of a rabbit hutch, passionately fond of animals...? He wondered about that. And all these years, if he was to believe her, Daphne had been deprived — in his selfishness he had prevented her from fulfilling her heart's desire!

Wandering into the drawing-room, where they sometimes had coffee after their meal, he came upon the box of jumble with 'Thy Servant a Dog' lying on top of it. Again his thoughts went back to childhood with some obscure memory of Daphne's confirmation,

50

though he could not have said why this particular object had brought it to mind. But it did make him think about the confirmation candidates of his own village and the arrangement that was to be made with the vicar of a neighbouring village to combine the two sets of classes. Tom knew in advance how it would work out – *he* would have to do all the work, for this particular fellow priest was skilled in the art of passing the buck. Perhaps he should ask Adam Prince's advice – he was sure *he* never got landed with anything he didn't want to do.

Delving in the jumble box, he took up 'Thy Servant a Dog' and contemplated it. Hadn't it been the title of a book by Kipling that had supplied that quotation? But Daphne wouldn't know, so all he said to her was, 'No reason why you shouldn't get a dog, is there? Why don't you do something about it?'

8

Martin Shrubsole was observing his mother-in-law. He sat opposite her, unconscious of the television programme that so absorbed her, yet not obviously making notes. He would not have wanted to hurt her feelings, though she was not, in his opinion, a particularly sensitive person.

Magdalen Raven was in her late sixties, short and inclined to be overweight, though Martin had succeeded in 'weaning' her away from sugar in tea and coffee, so that she now carried saccharine pellets in her handbag, in a little decorative container given to her by one of her grandchildren. Martin had also forbidden her to eat butter and now a plastic tub of some polyunsaturated preparation was placed by her at meals. Avice had been instructed to provide fresh fruit instead of puddings and to discourage her mother from taking a biscuit with her elevenses. In this way Martin was fulfilling his duty as a conscientious general practitioner and prescribing for his wife's mother just as he did for his older patients. But he did sometimes wonder whether he really wanted to preserve his mother-in-law all that much. She was a widow and Avice was her only child, and as she had now come to live with them the house was really too small for three adults and three children. At the moment it was out of the question for them to think of buying anything larger. Yet if Avice's mother were not so well looked after and preserved, if she were allowed all the white bread, sugar, butter, cakes and puddings that her naturally depraved taste craved, if – not to mince matters or to put too fine a point on it – she were to drop down dead, the Shrubsoles would have enough money to buy a larger house. This thought, instantly stifled, had more than once occurred to Martin in the watches of the night. But, of course, after it had occurred he became even more conscientious in the preservation of his mother-in-law. He was now more than a little worried at a report in one of the Sundays that certain types of artificial sweetener (in the U.S.A. of course) had been proved to cause cancer in mice. 'Couldn't you try taking tea and coffee without *any* sweetener?' he had suggested dutifully, but she didn't think she would like that at all. She had been quite definite in her reply. Not even in the war had she got to like tea without sugar, as so many people had.

Now, observing her in front of the television, wearing her new glasses, he was glad to note, her hair neatly set, her dried-up-looking hands with the short pink-varnished nails occupied with knitting for one of her grandchildren, Martin's natural kindness came out. 'Getting more used to those bi-focals, are you, mother?' he asked. 'I think you'll find it much better, not having to keep taking your glasses off all the time when you want to read your knitting pattern.'

Of course it was much better – everything about her son-in-law was 'better', Magdalen Raven knew this perfectly well. Good, better, best – and the best thing of all was that Martin had agreed that she should come and live with them now that the lease of her flat had run out – 'share their home', was the way people put it. She was lucky to have such a kind son-in-law, even if he wouldn't let her eat anything she really liked – everyone was agreed on that. And if some considered that her daughter made use of her as an unpaid nanny and baby-sitter, well, she loved the grandchildren, didn't she? What more could any woman want than to help to look after her grandchildren, her own flesh and blood after all. How many widows were so lucky? And tonight she wasn't even having to baby-sit, because there was going to be a sherry party – a 'drinks party', Avice called it. Christabel Gellibrand, the wife of the old doctor, had invited Magdalen Raven, without Avice and Martin, to introduce her to a few people in the village.

'Apparently she's asked that anthropologist woman – Emma Howick – remember, we saw her in her garden and you asked who she was?'

'Yes, what was she doing in the garden? I've forgotten.'

'Well, she wasn't *doing* anything,' said Avice impatiently. 'Just standing or picking something – it doesn't matter. But she's a newcomer to the village too, so it'll be nice for you to meet her.'

'And other people too, of course,' said Martin, noticing his mother-in-law's air of doubt. 'The rector and his sister, I should think – oh, and some ladies interested in local history. You remember we thought you might like to join up with them,' he added hopefully, for he and Avice had the idea that her mother might be usefully occupied in copying parish registers or something of that nature which, it was thought, might help to keep her brain in good trim, ticking over, as it were, rather than endlessly knitting and watching television. Very important that, Martin felt; he always made a point of advising his older patients to cultivate some intellectual interest.

'Well, that'll be nice,' said Magdalen, examining her nails. 'I think I'll just re-do these – what do you think?' She spread out her fingers.

'They look fine to me,' said Martin in a hearty tone. 'Not chipped at all.'

'Mummy, there's no time to do your nails,' said Avice. 'Martin, you'll take Mummy in the car, won't you?'

Martin agreed that he would, but 'Mummy' applied to Magdalen Raven did not come easily to him and he never used it. Nor could he bring himself to call her 'Magdalen', as she would have preferred. When he addressed her by name, other than just saying 'you', he called her 'mother', but that didn't seem quite right either, for she was not and never could be 'mother' to him.

It was surely better, Emma felt, *not* to know how one's doctor lived, not to tread on fine Persian rugs or to glimpse delicate porcelain and exquisite glass in an antique corner cupboard. But entering the graciously furnished hall of the Gellibrands' house – 'residence', one might almost say – Emma was surprised to detect underneath the scent of the lavender furniture polish a faint odour of tom cat – faint, certainly, but unmistakable. Then she remembered having seen a large black and white cat emerging from a shrubbery, head held high, a bird in his mouth. Presumably an unneutered tom, which would account for the smell. And hadn't Daphne said something about the old doctor only being interested in young people and babies and the general burgeoning of life? So he might well be against any interfering with Nature....

And now, it seemed, having come into the house the guests were directed to go out again through the drawing-room french windows on to a lawn, and forced or driven rather than encouraged to march along by an herbaceous border, commenting, admiring, enquiring. At the end of the border the garden turned into a kind of cultivated wilderness (bulbs in the spring, now over, of course, and later bluebells, the remains of which could be still seen). Some of the guests, who had put on their best shoes in honour of the party, seemed unwilling to progress beyond the lawn into the wild garden but they were driven on by their hostess and even down a rocky path to a pool where a water-lily, showing its first bud, demanded to be admired.

Emma, finding herself unable to comment adequately on this phenomenon, was glad to be diverted by a commotion behind her. Miss Grundy had stumbled and nearly fallen on the rocky path. She, the author of a romantic novel, had found herself in the kind of situation that might have provided a fruitful plot; but it was not the son of the house who came to her assistance or a handsome stranger but Emma, the anthropologist and observer of human behaviour. Ah, the sadness of life, she thought.

'Oh, Miss Grundy, are you all right? I was afraid you were going to fall.'

'It's these shoes — if I'd realised....'

Louis heels, they used to be called, Emma believed, as she helped Miss Grundy back up the path where Christabel G. was waiting at the top.

'I *told* you not to wear those shoes,' said Miss Lee to Miss Grundy, and Emma remembered how she had noticed Miss Lee's bossiness on other occasions. She supposed that when two people lived together one must always dominate or boss — Miss Lee over Miss Grundy, Daphne over Tom, perhaps Christabel G. over Dr G. She wasn't sure about the Shrubsoles or the Barracloughs; perhaps they had managed to achieve an equal partnership, though she suspected that Avice might boss her husband.

There was a general air of relief to be safely back indoors, for the party to begin 'properly'. A quick glance round the room told Emma that it was not a very interesting gathering, or at least it did not look to be, for most of the people standing round, clutching glasses of sherry or hoping to be offered one, were elderly and did not betray the fact that they might have led distinguished lives. She had heard that Mrs G. liked to give several parties each year and to divide her guests into suitable categories. She was not at all sure, even with her anthropological training, how this one should be classified. It might be that it was to serve as a warning to younger newcomers like herself and the Barracloughs — Emma had just seen Robbie and Tamsin enter the room — to remind them that they would be expected to keep their place, without attempting to make any changes or meddle with the traditions of village life as established by people like Mrs G. Or it could be just a gesture of welcome to newcomers, for she had noticed the young doctor's mother-in-law among the guests.

Emma saw that Mrs Dyer was in attendance, hovering with plates of crisps and small 'cocktail savouries'. As if to mark her appearance in a slightly different role, she had modified her dress for the occasion and was wearing a bright blue nylon overall and a smarter hat than usual, a maroon felt with a paste ornament in the form of an anchor. 'Fierce was the wild billow, dark was the night,' Emma thought, remembering a hymn from school days. 'Oars laboured heavily, foam glimmered white....'

Mrs Dyer thrust a plate towards her but Emma was loth to start eating before she had a glass in her hand and drink had not yet been offered to her. Standing uneasily – for no glass at all is even more awkward at a party than an empty glass – she suffered only a moment's embarrassment, for the rector, 'poor Tom', as she now found herself thinking of him, was at her side and offering her sherry.

'Dr G. has his hands full,' he explained, 'and Mrs Dyer doesn't really understand the first necessity at a party.'

Emma was grateful but the feeling wore off when he began to ask her about her 'work' and she was forced to explain about the urban study she had completed, and that led on to him asking her whether she intended to make a study of the village, the sort of question, half joking, that always followed when people knew what she did.

'I suppose I could study the village,' she said, 'but first of all I'd want to know what sort of a party this is – I believe there are various categories.'

Tom was a little taken aback by her frank way of speaking and hardly knew what to say. He did not like to tell Emma that the party on this occasion was not so much to welcome newcomers — though it was that in a sense — as to sort out in a social way sheep from goats and pick out various likely people to 'do' things in the village, above all to assist in the flower festival which Christabel was organising in the church. He could see her now, tall, thin and somehow menacing in her expensive flowered silk dress, peering about her like a bird about to swoop. He tried to melt into the background as Christabel bore down on Emma.

'Let me see now,' her voice rang out authoritatively, 'you were at Somerville, weren't you?'

'No,' said Emma. She hardly liked to say that she had taken her degree at the London School of Economics but did add that she was an anthropologist.

'Oh.' Christabel brushed aside anthropology and all its possible implications. 'Can you arrange flowers?' she asked.

'I suppose so....'

'Surely *all* ladies can arrange flowers,' said Adam Prince, sidling up to the little group.

'I'm thinking of the flower festival, of course,' said Christabel.

She had 'good bones', Emma thought, and had obviously once been beautiful — the worm in the bud, though that wasn't the kind of thought one could put into words at a sherry party. No doubt the mention of flowers had suggested the bud and the worm in it....

'So often in a cottage,' Adam Prince went on, 'one sees a simple bunch of wild flowers stuck into a jam jar.'

'Oh, Mr Prince, we shall want rather more than that,' said Christabel in a jovial tone. 'Dr Shrubsole's mother-in-law is going to help – she seems *very* keen. A nice little person – we must try to bring her into things now that she's come to live among us.'

'Yes, indeed,' said Tom, feeling that this was directed at him. He did not reveal that he was hoping to enlist Mrs Raven as a helper in some of his local history researches. A meek woman of retirement age could be of inestimable value, and he was glad to see that she was now deep in conversation with Miss Lee and Miss Grundy. They might even be discussing one of the 'projects' on which Mrs Raven might work.

'I'll *always* remember that Sunday morning,' Magdalen Raven was saying. 'Mr Chamberlain was to speak on the wireless – as we called it in those days – and my husband – of course he was alive then – kept saying that appeasement would *never* work. He always said Hitler wasn't to be trusted and of course he was quite right.'

'And the evacuees,' Miss Grundy broke in eagerly, 'do you remember the evacuees, and that mother who just sat up in bed smoking!'

'People smoked a lot in those days,' said Magdalen, almost with regret. 'Such funny cigarettes we had – do you remember Tenners, in a blue packet?' Smoking was, of course, another pleasure forbidden by her son-in-law. There were no ash-trays in the house.

'They used to say Hitler couldn't stand a long war,' said Miss Lee, 'but it seemed to go on *such* a long time, with that school in the manor and none of the family here in the village.'

'The family?' Magdalen asked.

'Yes, the girls and Miss Vereker, their governess, still trying to keep the mausoleum in order....'

'The mausoleum?' And the governess keeping it in order?

'Yes, by the church, you must have seen it, where some of the family are buried.'

'Oh, I must go there some time,' said Magdalen in a social way. Miss Lee seemed to be overcome by her memories and she tried to guide the conversation on to the days after the war when things weren't much better even though the fighting was over. 'Do you remember the meat ration going down to eightpence and that ewe mutton or whatever it was called?'

'Miss Vereker had a way with ewe mutton,' said Miss Lee, still on her memories. 'She was an imaginative cook....'

'I see you've been initiating Mrs Raven into our little group,' said Tom, coming up to them.

'Yes, we've been talking about the past,' said Miss Lee, 'something we all remember.' But her tone was slightly defiant and Tom knew that by 'the past' she did not mean quite what he did. Still, it was a beginning.

He looked around him to say something to Miss Howick — Emma, as he was beginning to think of her — but she had gone. He prepared to spend an evening with his sister, who had not been at the party, and to tell her 'all about it'.

61

9

One morning Tom went into the church, as he often did, to spend half an hour or so, not exactly to meditate or pray but to wander in a random fashion round the aisles, letting his thoughts dwell on various people in the village. This was in its way a kind of prayer, like bringing them into the church which so few of them actually visited, or never darkened its doors, as a more dramatic phrase had it. He studied the monuments and wall tablets, noticing repairs that were needed, brass that was tarnished (whose turn had it been last week?), and sometimes regretting Victorian additions to what had originally been a simple building.

The family at the manor had the largest and most interesting memorials, with florid inscriptions that taxed the memory of one's Latin. It was perhaps a pity that we no longer commemorated our dead in such terms, Tom felt, remembering the barer records of the twentieth century. Now a memorial more often took the form of an extension to the communion rails – a godsend indeed to old stiff knees – or a very plain tablet in chillingly good taste. We were more embarrassed nowadays or less insincere, he would not have liked to say which, for 'sincerity' was disproportionately valued today. It would be impossible, for example, to imagine anything

62

like the de Tankerville mausoleum being erected now. It had been put up outside the church in the early nineteenth century and later members of the family had been buried in it. Now, when they no longer lived at the manor, it seemed an awkward anachronism in such a small and humble parish.

Tom was thinking along these lines when he heard a movement at the back of the church. Somebody had come in, though whether visitor, parishioner or brass-cleaning lady he was unable to see. The 'person' – and in these days of sex equality and uniform dress and hairstyle the visitor could surely be so described – had moved into the de Tankerville chapel, as it was called, and appeared to be examining the monument of the recumbent crusader. As he came nearer, Tom saw that it was a young man with golden bobbed hair, dressed in the usual T-shirt and jeans and wearing pink rubber gloves, an unusual and slightly disturbing note.

Can I help you? Tom thought without in fact uttering the words, for it seemed at once too trivial and too profound an enquiry. An offer to 'help' might be taken literally when all that Tom felt himself capable of offering on this occasion was a brief history of the church and village with perhaps more detailed comments on some of the monuments, and he was about to start on his usual account when the young man forestalled him by speaking first.

'You must be the rector,' he said, rather too effusively, almost as if he were congratulating Tom on having got the job. 'I'm Terry Skate – I've come to see your mausoleum. I thought I'd just nip into the church first, to put me in the picture – if you see what I mean – get to know the general set-up, what was involved and all that.'

The two of them were standing looking down at the effigy of Sir Hubert de Tankerville. Tom felt that it might almost have been his fault, as if Mr Skate might blame him in some way, that the head of one of the little dogs reposing at the crusader's feet was broken off. Contemplating the headless animal, he thought of the Puritans and the Civil War, but again the visitor got in first with a comment about vandalism, 'even in olden times'.

'You haven't been here before?' Tom said, trying to remember the others who had come periodically to 'see to' the mausoleum, mostly grey elderly men, certainly nobody like Terry Skate.

'No, it's my first visit, the first of *many*, I hope. My friend and I have taken over this florist's, you see – of course we have lots of regular orders for floral displays, not to mention weddings and funerals, you name it, we do it – but we've never done a mausoleum before.'

'What exactly are you going to do?'

'Oh, just tidy it up – it's more a job for a garden centre, really – supply new plants and bulbs for the outside, daffs at Easter and that kind of thing. Being a church person myself I got the job, my friend being agnostic.'

'I see. Then you are....' Tom had been going to say 'one of us' until he realised the possible ambiguity of the phrase. Besides, it was most unlikely that Terry Skate's churchgoing would have anything in common with the simple village service which was all that Tom's parishioners would tolerate.

'Goodness, yes! Choirboy, server, M.C. even – you name it.... You'd have to be a believer, wouldn't you, to do a mausoleum?'

Tom saw that this must be so and proceeded to give a

brief history of the mausoleum – how it had been put up in 1810 to commemorate a de Tankerville killed in the Peninsular War, and how later members of the family had been buried there and monuments erected to them.

'Could we have a peep inside?' Terry asked enthusiastically. 'I'm just longing to see.'

They went out of the church, unlocked the gate of the mausoleum and folded back the grille leading to the interior. A heavy red velvet curtain had to be drawn aside to reveal the box-like tombs and monuments. Although it was a warm day outside, the icy white of the marble and the cold blind faces of the classical sculptures struck very chill, and Tom shivered. He did not often go into the mausoleum and was unable to match Terry's enthusiastic comments, disliking the whole concept and finding the marble representations pretentious and unsympathetic.

Terry agreed that it was cold inside. 'You'd think you could put a storage heater or even a paraffin stove in here,' he suggested.

'Oh, I don't think that would be suitable,' said Tom. 'Anyway, nobody really goes inside now – nobody spends much time here,' he added, aware that he was saying something slightly comic. 'There's nobody left of the family to take any interest.' This was sad, of course, though more from the historical than the human point of view. There were documents lost for ever to the local historian. If only he could have been here in the thirties when the de Tankervilles left the manor!

'Has the family died out?' Terry asked.

Tom explained its history, the last surviving male killed in the Great War with no dependants, the sisters selling the house not long after that, the present owner a

65

man who took no interest in the village.... The chill of the mausoleum was beginning to get into his bones. Should he ask Terry Skate back to the rectory for a cup of coffee?

They went outside and into the little garden surrounding the edifice where there were some gravestones with spaces for vases of flowers or pot plants.

'I suppose it was done at Whit and somebody's taken away the dead flowers.'

'Yes, one of the flower ladies usually does that.'

'Which is more than she did in the church, if I may make so bold,' said Terry with a laugh.

'Yes, something does seem to have been neglected there,' Tom agreed. 'And of course mid-week is a bad time for flowers.'

'Dead flowers left in the water make such a stink.'

'Lilies that fester smell far worse than weeds,' Tom suggested.

'These weren't lilies – larkspurs, I should think. I might get some pelargoniums for the graves here,' Terry went on. 'A splash of colour – that's what's needed.'

'I'm sure that will be admirable,' Tom said.

'I've got some plants in the van. Meanwhile, is there a café or teashop in the village?'

Tom was dismayed, for of course there was nothing of the kind and it was too early for the pub. It would have to be the rectory after all. He apologised for the lack and extended his invitation.

'Oh, that *is* kind – I was hoping you'd say that. I almost prayed there wouldn't be a café in the village and that I'd have a chance to see inside your beautiful old rectory.'

66

'There's not much to see,' said Tom, again apologetic, 'though of course it is an old house.'

'Monks lived there, perhaps?' Terry suggested.

'Well, no — I don't think there is any evidence of that....'

'But it's what I'd like to think. There's a definitely monastic feeling here,' said Terry, glancing critically round the hall and taking in its shabbiness.

The hall was sparsely furnished, certainly, but the appearance of Daphne and Mrs Dyer struck an unmonastic note.

'What about some coffee?' Tom asked.

'We've had ours,' said Mrs Dyer firmly. 'We're turning out the dining-room today.'

'What about a glass of sherry then?' Tom turned to Terry, who was taking in the scene. 'Or is it too early for you?'

'Oh, I'll make some coffee,' said Daphne, coming forward, but it was too late — sherry had been offered and there was no going back.

Tom introduced Terry Skate to his sister and explained about the mausoleum.

'Oh, how splendid — to have somebody who really cares about it, especially now, with the flower festival.' Daphne was enthusiastic.

'Flower festival — in your church? You don't say!'

Tom wondered if Terry was being impertinent but decided that he was a guileless young man expressing himself in his natural way.

'You'll have to get rid of those dead flowers,' Terry joked.

'Yes — whose turn was it last week?' Tom asked, trying to introduce a sterner note.

'Was it the third Sunday?' Daphne mused. 'Yes it was, wasn't it. It was Mrs Broome's turn.'

'But....' Tom protested.

'Yes – she's in hospital – had a heart attack last week.' Daphne let out a peal of unexpected laughter. 'So no wonder the flowers look a bit off colour!'

'I see – but I didn't think Mrs Broome ever came to church.'

'No, but she's always done the flowers on the third Sunday – ever since we've been here.'

Tom let this pass without comment – obviously he had failed somewhere.

'Your church would lend itself to something special in the way of flower arrangements,' said Terry hopefully.

'Oh, it will be just flowers from people's gardens,' said Tom quickly, fearing that Terry might expect to get an order for expensive florist's blooms. 'This time of year there ought to be plenty.'

'I must pop over,' Terry said, 'when you have it. You could get a lovely effect on that crusader – pity about the dog's head being broken off, though, but you might conceal it with a posy.' He stood up. 'Thanks for the sherry, rector. I must say, I like a sweet sherry in the morning.'

Tom said nothing. It had been a medium dry but not, of course, Spanish, and the bottle seemed sadly depleted since the last time he had drunk from it. Did Daphne sometimes indulge, to compensate for not having a dog? He found himself wondering if his morning had been wasted but was prepared to believe that it might not have been. God did still move in a mysterious way, even in this day and age or at this 'moment in time', as some of his parishioners might have said.

68

10

'COFFEE MORNING AND BRING-AND-BUY SALE
AT YEW TREE COTTAGE. TUESDAY. 10.30.
ADMISSION 15p.'

Meditating on the note which had been pushed
through her letter-box, Emma wondered whether a
serious sociological study had ever been made of this
important feature of village life. Miss Lee and Miss
Grundy were holding a coffee morning at their cottage
(and there *was* a yew tree at the side of the house). And
the clergyman in the photograph on the piano, wearing
an exceptionally high clerical collar, was Canon
Grundy, Miss Grundy's father, sometime Anglican
chaplain on the Riviera. This much Emma gathered
when she entered the sitting-room, but from then on
there was such a confusion of impressions that
afterwards she found herself making notes under
headings, almost as if she were indeed preparing a paper
for a learned society.

In aid of what? was her first note. This was not
specified on the invitation and nobody mentioned any
particular cause, it being assumed that everybody
already knew. It might have been something in aid of
Old People (Elderly or Aged, however you liked to put

it), or children, or the Cats' Protection League (unlikely), or a political party (Conservative or Liberal, *not* Labour), Shelter or Oxfam, or just the vague all-embracing 'Church Funds'. (Or just not in aid of anything?)

Entrance. The 15p. entrance fee (placed in a hand-made pottery bowl on a small table in the doorway) included a cup of coffee and a biscuit, and a piece of home-made cake could be bought for 10p. Miss Lee and Miss Grundy served the coffee, assisted by a number of willing ladies (rather too many), mostly grey-haired and elderly. (Far more than might have been thought necessary for the serving of a cup of rather weak coffee.)

Participants, e.g. others present not engaged in coffee-making. (a) Men. None. (b) Women. Daphne Dagnall; Avice Shrubsole and her mother Magdalen Raven; old Miss Lickerish (didn't seem quite to fit into the social hierarchy – so was the coffee morning perhaps in aid of some animal charity?); Tamsin Barraclough (didn't quite fit either, so perhaps she was also making a social survey?!); Christabel G. (made brief visit, more in nature of royal personage bestowing a favour). Various other women, unidentified, possibly from neighbouring villages.

Bring and Buy. Everybody brought something, mostly jam, pickle, cake, biscuits or scones, all home-made. Impossible to discover who exactly had contributed what (expect that Miss Lickerish was seen to deposit a tin of baked beans on the table). The bringing and buying, consisting as it did of people bringing what they had made and buying what somebody else had made, achieved a kind of village exchange system, some coming off better than others. No doubt there was plenty of criticism of others' efforts, even if not openly

70

expressed – who, for example, was the bringer of the not-quite-right marmalade which had been boiled past the setting point and gone syrupy? Whoever it was could have saved face by buying it back herself and in the general bustle this ruse might not be spotted. Christabel G.'s contribution was a cut above the ordinary plum and rhubarb jams – a pot of quince jam (labelled 'Quince Preserve'). Emma quickly bought this, having contributed only half a dozen scones herself – a bargain.

The raffle. Apparently this was an essential feature of a bring-and-buy sale ('We always have one'). Various objects were displayed on top of the piano round the photograph of Canon Grundy. These objects (or 'prizes') were: a large iced cake; a flowered toilet hold-all in shades of mauve and pink; a small tray decorated with an engraving of Lake Como (or Maggiore); a set of pottery mugs; a tea-towel patterned with Scottie dogs. Tickets (3 for 10p.) had been sold in advance.

All was ready for the draw, there was even an expectant hush in the room, for this was a kind of climax to the morning, when Adam Prince made a sudden and dramatic appearance bearing a bottle of wine.

Emma had been thinking that no man would dare to attend the sale but then she realised that, of course, there could be exceptions. A former Anglican priest might well have the sort of courage required for the occasion and Adam, so very much at ease with ladies, obviously came into this category.

'Just something for the raffle,' he murmured. 'I do hope I'm not too late and that you'll find this not too unacceptable.'

He was gone before he could be thanked, leaving Miss

Lee grasping, embracing almost, the very dark-looking bottle of wine.

'Oh dear,' was her first reaction.

'*Red* wine,' said Miss Grundy. 'But how kind of him,' she added.

'Fancy him coming in his car,' Daphne said. 'You'd have thought he could have walked those few steps from his front door.'

'I suppose we must put this in for the raffle,' said Miss Lee, hovering uncertainly with the bottle still clasped to her bosom.

'Of course,' said Avice, moving some of the other objects on the piano aside to make room for the bottle. 'And I think we ought to get going with the draw,' she added bossily. 'Some of us haven't got all morning to spend in chat.'

Emma felt humbled, as if the reproach might have been directed at her own conversational efforts. Spending all the morning in chat could well apply to the anthropologist who gathered so much of his material in this way.

'Yes, we must,' said Miss Lee. 'We'll take it in turns to draw and the winning ticket has first choice of the prizes.'

Daphne's ticket was the first to be drawn and she chose the iced cake; then came Avice's mother, who chose the tray. Other prize-winners followed, each choosing something until, rather to Emma's surprise, only the bottle of wine was left. The fortunate person with the last ticket was unknown to her – a thin, nervous-looking middle-aged woman in a pale blue Courtelle dress, who seemed to shrink away from the bottle, so dark and menacing, which was to be her prize.

'Lucky you,' said Emma feelingly.

'Oh, I don't drink, really,' murmured the woman, 'though I've no objection to other people....'

'Why don't we give Mrs Furse another prize,' said Avice, 'and put the bottle in again?' She looked round the room in search of something that might make an acceptable substitute, her glance even seeming to light on the photograph of Canon Grundy in his high collar. 'Perhaps, Miss Lee...?'

'*I* know,' said Miss Lee, going out of the room and reappearing with a tissue-paper wrapped parcel, 'perhaps Mrs Furse would like this.'

It was a small mirror with a floral decoration round the edges.

'Barbola work, isn't it?' said somebody.

The mirror was accepted, examined and admired and the raffle was drawn again. This time Avice Shrubsole won the bottle and bore it away in triumph – the bring-and-buy had been worthwhile. Her mother had also enjoyed the morning and there was a slight feeling of guilt mingled with her enjoyment, for she had mislaid her saccharine tablets and taken two lumps of sugar in her coffee as well as eating a slice of home-made sandwich cake with cream and jam filling.

Emma wished she had won the wine, but she had the quince preserve and a plastic bag containing six rock buns, so perhaps the morning had not been wasted. She had also gathered material for a note on an important village activity. Then she realised that Miss Lickerish was walking just behind her, so she turned back and tried to engage her in conversation, feeling that she might contribute some fragment of historical or sociological interest.

'I see the young doctor's wife took the bottle,' Miss Lickerish said, initiating the conversation.

'Yes, it was good of Mr Prince to give a prize,' Emma said.

'Well, he wouldn't miss it, would he.'

'No, perhaps not, but still....'

They walked on in silence for a while, then Emma, making some trite remark about the fine weather, found that she had started Miss Lickerish off on a confused rambling about summer-time, the long light evenings, a ruined cottage in the woods and the goings-on there at some unspecified time in the past. Obviously the bottle of wine combined with the idea of summer weather had started some train of thought in the old woman's mind that Emma was unable to follow.

When they reached the door of Miss Lickerish's cottage Emma looked in through the window and saw a cat on the kitchen table, eating something out of a dish that might or might not have been what the animal was intended to eat.... She said goodbye to the old woman and returned home in a state of some confusion.

Back at Yew Tree Cottage Miss Lee and Miss Grundy set about clearing up the aftermath of the coffee morning and bring-and-buy sale which had made a shambles of their drawing-room. They went about their task in silence, an efficient one on Miss Lee's part – 'Let's get this mess tidied up, shall we?' But Miss Grundy's silence was a hurt one – Miss Lee had taken the barbola mirror without asking her permission and it had been a present to *both* of them. Another source of quiet resentment on her part.

11

People's attitudes towards the flower festival were 'ambivalent', Emma thought, the jargon word coming into her mind. Everybody knew about it, of course, could hardly fail to, with notices plastered all over the village, but there had never been such a thing in the old days. Flower arrangement was a fashionable modern pastime for a certain type of woman – a hobby for the gentler sex, almost like the accomplishments of a Victorian young lady – and even though the art of arranging flowers may have originated in Japan, it was now an unmistakably English activity. The chaste positioning of a single bloom or spray in the Oriental manner would be seen as totally inadequate in the present setting; much more would be expected. Emma liked the idea of a single dark red rose or peony in a pottery jug against the grey stone of the church, but knew better than to suggest it. Her own garden could provide a few delphiniums and lupins and there was a pink climbing rose on the front of the cottage. She was just in the act of cutting down some branches of this when she saw Tom approaching with Adam Prince.

'What a charming picture you make, with the roses,' said Adam smoothly.

Emma tried to think of a gracious answer to this

rather obvious compliment. Then, before she had been able to produce anything, Tom, suddenly and ridiculously, burst into poetry.

'The two divinest things this world has got
A lovely woman in a rural spot,'

he recited.

There was a brief stunned silence, surely one of dismay, then Emma broke it by laughing. The two men must surely realise that she certainly wasn't lovely, not even pretty.

'Leigh Hunt,' said Tom quickly, attempting to cover up his foolishness. '*Not* a good poem.'

He was hardly improving matters – there had been no need to make that kind of critical judgement. 'I thought of taking a few flowers along to the church,' Emma said. 'Mrs G. does want things out of people's gardens, doesn't she?'

'I like to watch ladies arranging flowers,' Adam said. 'It was one of the aspects of my calling that I most enjoyed.'

Tom thought this an unusual way of looking on the duties of a parish priest, but made no comment. After all, his own most enjoyable aspect was concerned with delving into parish registers, which seemed little better than watching ladies arranging flowers. 'Did you ever have a flower festival in your church?' he asked Adam.

'Oh, I think so – but I was so often away in the summer.'

Tom expressed surprise.

'Yes, I usually managed to avoid parish summer occasions – fêtes, and that kind of thing – couldn't stand them,' said Adam smugly.

76

'But how did you manage to "avoid" them, as you put it?'

'By arranging to be on holiday and out of the country – in Italy, for preference.' Adam laughed. 'You ought to try it.'

Tom in his bewilderment could think of no answer to this. 'Arranging to be in Italy' at the time of the flower festival – if only he could!

The three of them had now reached the church where Mrs G. was directing operations.

'Ah, Miss Hislop,' she said, giving Emma the wrong name, 'how kind, bringing flowers too. So *many* delphiniums, one hardly knows....'

What on earth to do with them, Emma thought, completing the sentence. She glanced beyond Christabel G. to where a group of women she did not at once recognise were doing things with flowers and even branches of trees. Then she saw that Miss Lee and Miss Grundy were among them, also Dr Shrubsole's mother-in-law and even Mrs Dyer, though the last was just filling vases with water from the tap outside. Would she be allowed to participate in the actual arrangement? Emma wondered. There might be material for a note on village status here. And was the festival itself in some way connected with fertility, perhaps? Looking again at the assembled group of ladies, she doubted this interpretation. It was a mistake to suppose that every human activity was related to sex, whatever Freud might say.

Seeing one of the doctor's cats scratching in the shrubbery, Daphne found herself dredging up another Greek memory, this time of an early morning in Delphi

77

when, looking down towards Itea, she had seen in a field far below a little cat scratching in the earth in the timeless manner of cats everywhere.

'My wife has already gone to the church,' said Dr G., coming out of the house with a black and white tom cat on his shoulder. 'And how are you these days?' he asked Daphne, almost as if he thought he was in the surgery and obliged to make such an enquiry.

'Oh fine, thanks,' said Daphne, embarrassed because she had deserted the old doctor.

'Martin looking after you all right?'

'Dr Shrubsole? Oh yes — thank you.'

'Still want to get away to a Greek island?' Dr G. asked, in a mocking, jovial tone.

Daphne smiled but did not answer. Ought not her longing to have been a secret, or did everyone in the village know anyway? 'I'd better be getting along to the church,' she said.

'Well, take care of yourself, my dear,' said Dr G. 'We all get a bit low at times. Nothing to worry about. Get yourself a new hat — that's what I always say.' He chuckled and bent down to allow the cat to descend from his shoulder.

He *did* think he was in the surgery, Daphne realised. What a good thing she had transferred to Martin Shrubsole, especially now that she was getting older. Martin had made a special study of geriatrics — nasty word, but we all came to it. He would look after her, but then she might not be here all that much longer to *be* looked after. Her friend Heather Blenkinsop was coming at the weekend, to visit the flower festival, of course, but also to discuss final plans for their holiday. Who knew what that might lead to? Not a beach hut on Mykonos, of course. Those were all the rage a few years ago, but that wasn't the sort of thing that would suit Heather and herself. Perhaps one of the other more remote islands, comparatively undeveloped....

How big the church was, she thought, as the building loomed in sight. The Victorians were ridiculously ostentatious, even with their larger congregations, adding to the unpretentious old structure in the way her brother Tom deplored. In Greece, certainly in the country places, they had those miniature white-washed churches, almost like something made out of a child's bricks....

'Shall I do my usual window?' she asked, confronting Mrs G.

'Your usual window....' Mrs G., her arms full of lilies, spoke absently, as if she hardly remembered who Daphne was. It was hurtful, that kind of thing. Tears came into Daphne's eyes as she stood there, waiting to be told what to do. 'Oh, I think we're going to do a bit more than our usual windows,' Christabel said. 'After all, it *is* a festival, isn't it?'

Daphne realised that she hated flower arranging altogether. Sometimes she hated the church too, wasn't sure that she even believed any more, though of course one didn't talk about that kind of thing. And Christabel G. hadn't told her what she was to do, just snubbed her and left her standing uselessly by a heap of greenery. Into Daphne's mind came yet another Greek vignette, the memory of an old man on the seashore bashing an octopus against a stone....

'I wonder if this is all right?' Magdalen Raven was asking Daphne's opinion. 'These tall branches keep falling over, but I don't like to make them shorter. Mrs

79

Gellibrand said she wanted the effect of *height* — I suppose I could put crumpled wire-netting in the bottom — that might do.... It's going to be *lovely*, isn't it?' Martin had suggested that she might like to go along and help at the church even though she wasn't as yet on the flower-arranging rota, and she was really enjoying herself in spite of not being able to get the branches of beech leaves to stand up properly. 'Getting involved' was one of Martin's favourite prescriptions for the approach of old age, the beginning of the end of life. But in a sense we were all 'involved', weren't we, always had been. 'Do you remember?' she wanted to say to Daphne, hoping to share a few more wartime memories, but before she could put her thoughts into words somebody had brought her a green plastic substance to prop up the branches and she had to get on with the business in hand.

It certainly did look lovely, Emma decided on the day of the festival, though not quite like a church. The arrangements were too elaborate, too much like the foyer of an advertising agency or an expensive block of flats or the decorations for a smart wedding. But what exactly *did* one want? Simple arrangements of cow-parsley and campion or bunches of drooping bluebells in jam jars? Perhaps not flowers at all, ancient grey stone set off by the austerity of Lent?

'Well, I must say it's an improvement on the last time I was here.' Unknown to Emma, Terry Skate and a friend had come into the side chapel and were contemplating the crusader effigy and the dog with its head broken off. 'But they haven't taken my advice — *I* told them they could conceal the damage with a posy of small flowers – forget-me-nots and moss roses would be just the job – but they didn't want to know....'

Emma had noticed the broken dog's head, but to her it was a pathetic, even romantic, touch rather than something to be concealed with a posy of flowers. And after all, one must remember that it was history. She was just about to point this out to the young man when she noticed another man in a rather long raincoat standing in one of the side aisles, examining a wall tablet rather than the elaborate arrangement of peonies and delphiniums behind him. Why was he wearing a raincoat on this beautiful summer day? she wondered. The first lines of a Shakespeare sonnet came into her mind,

> Why didst thou promise such a beauteous day
> And make me travel forth without my cloak?

But this was the other way round, for the day was already beauteous and there was no need for any kind of cloak, certainly not a raincoat. She concealed herself behind the delphiniums and studied the man more closely. When he turned round she saw that it was Graham Pettifer. There was a kind of bent look about the shoulders which might explain why she had not recognised him immediately. She could not run away and hide or pretend she had not seen him, if that was what she wanted to do, for in her confusion she hardly knew what she wanted. Obviously she must face him and find out why he had come in this unexpected way.

'Why, Graham....' She feigned surprise.

'Emma, I had to come....' He moved towards her, arms outstretched, as if about to embrace her.

Not *here*, she thought, backing away from him and

81

almost knocking over the peonies and delphiniums. The church was full of people, strolling round admiring the flower arrangements.

'I don't seem to have eaten since yesterday,' he said surprisingly.

'But why not?' This was really too much.

'I couldn't, somehow – things have been too upsetting – I didn't feel like food.'

'You'd like to eat something now, perhaps?' Emma suggested. It was a little after three o'clock, so an early tea, provided by Daphne with Miss Lee and Miss Grundy in the rectory garden, was a possibility, or would a late lunch be more appropriate? If 'things' had been 'upsetting' it was most likely that Graham would be unable to specify any particular meal, but tea – always tea – and a boiled egg and toast might be suitable, she thought, and this was what she began to prepare when they returned to her cottage.

Graham sat slumped in a chair, not speaking but fixing his gaze on various objects in the room, almost as if he were noticing dust or some other displeasing aspect.

'Two eggs?' Emma asked. 'And how do you like them?'

'Oh, just as they come.'

'Boiled eggs don't exactly do that.' On the hard side, then, she thought, five minutes. A too-soft-boiled egg would be awkward to manage, slithering all over the place in the way they did. Not to be coped with by a person in an emotional state, though Mr Woodhouse in that novel about her namesake had claimed that it was not unwholesome. 'I'll have some toast too,' she said, 'to keep you company.' It was hardly the weather for toast but it seemed easier.

'Aren't you going to have a boiled egg then?'

'No, I've had lunch.' She wished he would explain his presence here a little more fully, but whatever urge had driven him to seek her company now seemed to have evaporated. 'Did something happen?' she asked at last. 'Did Claudia...?'

'I suppose you could say that. Ah, this is good!' He had cracked open one of the eggs and was spooning out the richly yellow yolk on to a piece of toast.

Emma was relieved to see that the egg was perfectly done, with the white firm and the yolk just runny enough.

'Free range, are they?' he went on. 'I suppose they would be, in the country. It's so *good* to be here, free-range eggs and all – just what I need.'

Daphne's friend, Heather Blenkinsop, arrived in her little yellow car and parked outside the church. She was a short dumpy woman of fifty-nine but she looked a good deal younger and smarter than Daphne, wearing her usual garments of Welsh tweed trousers and matching cape. She rather liked Tom and wished she could have gone up to him with a kiss, as older people tended to do nowadays – a new fashion, not perhaps meaning very much but, in her opinion, a pleasant one. But Tom was standing in the church porch to welcome visitors and discreetly draw attention to the large glass bottle which had been placed in the doorway for donations. It was already quite full of ten- and fifty-pence pieces and there were even a few folded notes.

Tom had been hoping to come upon Emma in the church – surely she would put in an appearance at the flower festival if only for its anthropological interest? –

and was disappointed when he learned that she had been seen leaving the church – he must have missed her somehow – in the company of a man. What man could this be? he wondered. She was perfectly entitled to number men among her friends – it might even be a brother, though he had always understood that she was Beatrix Howick's only child....

'Ah, Heather – good to see you....' Tom did not care for his sister's friend very much, though he respected her as a librarian, even if her interest in local history appeared a little excessive at times and there was something forced and unnatural about her frequent references to the sites of deserted medieval villages and the appearance of ridge and furrow in the landscape. Could any normal woman be quite so interested? he sometimes wondered, conscious that he was being unfair to Heather. He could have wished that Emma might show a bit more interest, might express a desire to study rent rolls or help in his search for the site of their D.M.V. Instead of which she had been seen to leave the church with a strange man, some anthropologist, no doubt.

'Before I forget, Tom,' Heather was saying, 'I came across a very interesting new book on hedge-dating the other day – something right up your street – a completely new theory....'

Tom murmured a polite acknowledgement. He was not particularly interested in hedge-dating.

Emma had been glad when Graham suggested a drink at the pub, for it seemed that the suddenness of his impulse had made him forget the original reason for his coming. He had said that it was good to be with her but no further explanation was offered and Emma did not yet feel that she had progressed far enough in their revived relationship to demand anything more. So, after the ritual cup of tea, the ritual comfort of the pub, the drink, the cosy atmosphere, the company.

It was not a notably cosy pub, its old shabby interior having been refurbished in the early sixties so that it was now shabby in a different, less attractive, way. Mr Spears, the landlord, was behind the bar, talking to Geoffrey Poore, who played the organ in church and sat in the pub most evenings drinking Guinness. There was a group of old village men in one corner and in another Mrs Dyer's son Jason with a girl. Silence fell when Emma and Graham entered and went up to the bar to order their drinks – gin and tonic for Emma and a pint of the local bitter for Graham. They settled at an empty table and began to make conversation in a stilted way, asking the assembled company if they had been to the flower festival, what they thought of it, what a blessing it had been such a fine day. The response was uncertain and in some way obscurely hostile. Mr Spears did venture to observe that they had never had such a thing in the old days and the organist supposed that it gave the ladies something to occupy themselves with. Mrs Dyer's son and his girl said nothing, nor did the old village men. It was a relief when Robbie and Tamsin Barraclough came in and Emma and Graham could invite them to their corner and start their own conversation. The other people in the pub also began to talk more freely among themselves and there was a noticeable lightening of the atmosphere.

'I wonder what significance the festival has had in the cycle of village life,' Emma muttered, with a quick glance at the old men sitting like some group of primitive sculpture.

'I suppose it can't have the same impact as a West African festival or even a European peasant fiesta,' said Robbie. 'I should guess it has had no effect whatsoever on this group assembled here.'

'But on the other women living here, the middle-class ladies, the rivalry and all that,' said Tamsin.

'Especially anything connected with the church,' Graham pointed out.

He began to talk sociological shop with the Barracloughs, teasing Tamsin in an almost flirtatious way, so that Emma found herself considering the festival and its significance in a different, less scientific, light. Flowers in a beautiful setting and a meeting with an old lover suggested a romantic novel rather than a paper for a learned society. But she had never thought of writing fiction, had, indeed, tended to despise her mother's studies of the Victorian novel. Now, however, she found herself wondering how the evening was going to end.

'I'm sorry,' Graham said when they were back in the cottage, 'I seem to have left it a bit late to get back tonight.'

Surely he was not afraid to drive in the dark? Or was it inconvenient in some other way? How was she to interpret his meaning?

'Would it cause a scandal in the village if I stayed here? I suppose I should have asked at the pub — they probably have rooms?'

'I don't know if anyone ever stays there. I do have a spare room.'

'Oh, fine — if you don't mind.'

'Of course not – would you like a drink?' Emma had almost said 'nightcap', the kind of thing associated with milkiness and a generally more cosy atmosphere than that obtaining between them at this moment.

'Nothing for me, thanks.'

They were standing in the spare room, side by side, not touching. Emma realised that Graham was not quite as tall as she was – had it always been like that or had he shrunk, diminished, in some way?

He made no move towards her but stroked the cover of the divan bed admiringly. 'William Morris, isn't it?'

'Yes, Golden Lily I think it's called. Goodnight then.'

'Goodnight.'

Nothing more was said and it was only as she lay in bed, going over the events of the day, that Emma wondered what he would do about a toothbrush or pyjamas.

Next day he went off early, after coffee and a piece of toast, as if ashamed of having come at all. He thanked Emma for her 'hospitality' but did not kiss her goodbye. No further mention was made of his marital difficulties and no further meeting promised.

The Sunday evening of the festival Tom preached about heaven, or what people's idea of heaven might be. It seemed a bold and imaginative, perhaps even appropriate, subject to choose, with all the flower arrangements still surrounding the congregation, as if they were already translated into that blessed state.

Emma noticed Sir Miles sitting in the usual manor pew, or rather the pew that would have been the usual one had he attended the church more often. He had a party with him, two women in smart flowered silk summer dresses, a girl wearing a long Laura Ashley pink-and-white print skirt, and a young man with fair wavy hair, gazing around him as if he had never been in a church before.

'We each of us have our own idea of heaven,' Tom declared, and immediately Emma's own picture came into her mind, dating from school days – the Almighty, a nebulous figure, and seated on his right her headmistress, eyes gleaming but kindly behind rimless glasses which in an earlier age would have been pince-nez. This reminded her that her mother was coming to stay next week, bringing with her an old college friend who was a headmistress, so the whole idea of 'heaven' took on a different aspect. Not that one thought about heaven all that much now – certainly the events of the previous evening had done nothing to turn Emma's thoughts towards it.

'What a pity we can't have flowers like this in the church *always*,' people were saying as they said goodnight to Tom, with a hint of reproach, as if he should have seen to it.

Emma slipped past him, not wanting to have that kind of conversation. She wondered why she had come to church, for it had not been to have another look at the flowers.

12

Emma never felt completely at ease with Isobel
Mound, her mother's old college friend, for in spite of
her friendly manner there was about her just a suspicion of the stern glint of eyes behind pince-nez, even
though she wore modishly shaped glasses whose light
brown frames toned perfectly with her soft, carefully
tinted hair. Perhaps any headmistress, however up to
date, would inevitably remind Emma of her first one,
seated on the right hand of the Almighty in heaven.

Isobel was to sleep in the spare room where Graham
had spent the night of the flower festival, with Morris
wallpaper and matching bedspread – the golden lilies
rioting (unsuitably, as it turned out) – a carafe of fresh
water on the bedside table, and a selection of
paperbacks with covers that could offend nobody. The
room looked out over the garden and beyond that to a
field where, in the days when no one bothered about
such things, a regrettable corrugated-iron structure had
been erected by the owner to house livestock. Now, of
course, it spoilt the view, though age and decay had
given it a certain antique interest as a relic of the thirties
when the village had been poor and tumbledown.

Emma's mother Beatrix would be in her usual room,

with the bookshelves filled with novels by Charlotte M. Yonge and other lesser Victorians and the desk in the window looking out over the village street. Beatrix liked to sit here hoping to witness the kind of events that might have taken place a hundred years ago, but more often than not she was disappointed.

A small supper party had been planned for one of the evenings when Isobel would be there, and Tom and Daphne had been invited. Then, feeling that Tom might not be completely at ease with *four* women, even though he was a clergyman and one of the women was his sister, Emma invited Adam Prince to join the party. His inclusion meant that the choosing of the menu caused her more anxiety than usual, though she did not know whether he was as critical of food eaten in private houses as of that offered to him in the course of his 'work'. As the party was to be on a Friday, there was the possibility that fish might have to be provided. Were the clergy, or Roman Catholic laymen, still obliged to eat fish on a Friday? Emma wondered.

'Fish is now regarded as a luxury,' Beatrix said. 'I'm sure Tom would be the last person to expect fish on a Friday.'

'But Adam Prince – a Catholic convert, an Anglican turned Roman,' said Emma uneasily, '*and* an inspector of high-class eating places – he might well look on fish as no more than his due.'

'What is the rule for Roman Catholics these days?' Isobel asked. 'One wouldn't want to be shown up as ignorant, not knowing....'

'Not *au fait* with what the form is in Rome,' Emma prompted, 'though *we* could hardly be expected to know the secrets of the Vatican kitchens.'

'Still, it might be a graceful compliment to Adam to provide a fish dish of some kind,' said Beatrix.

But what kind of fish? The usual pie made of coley would hardly do, though it could no doubt be disguised in a suitable sauce, mushroom or shrimp. In the end Emma made a tuna fish mousse, and a French onion tart with a salad, to be followed by various cheeses and ice cream from the village shop. After all, it was only supper, and lobsters − which Adam might have expected at some of the places he visited − were not easily obtainable in a West Oxfordshire village.

Entering Emma's sitting-room with his sister, Tom found himself confronted by the three women, not one of whom − in his eyes − looked immediately attractive, though he was of course aware that he must look below the surface. He did not take in as much detail as a woman would have done, but the general effect was unpleasing.

Emma was in a drab black and grey cotton which reminded him of a servant's morning dress of the old days − the sort of thing she would do the fires in or the front doorstep. Beatrix wore a dress of dark brownish-patterned silky material, its small collar pinned with a heavy Victorian brooch set with an ugly pebble-like stone. Isobel was in a beige crêpe two-piece, in rather boringly good taste − she must have chosen it for speech day or some other school function − she wore a necklace of seed pearls and small earrings to match, also new shoes that looked as if they might be uncomfortable. As for Daphne, Tom had long ceased to regard his sister as a woman whose clothes might be worthy of notice, sometimes he hardly even thought of her as a human being. In fact she was wearing a

91

pink-flowered cotton dress, rather too short by present standards, but she was saving her better clothes for her Greek holiday.

The offering of sherry was achieved before Adam Prince arrived, with apologies for being late, if he *was* late. His way of putting it made Tom feel that he and Daphne had been a little too early, but he was used to Adam's ways, and he was not surprised that when they sat down to eat it should be Adam who complimented Emma, rather too fulsomely it seemed for such a detail, on the exquisite thinness of the sliced cucumber with which she had decorated the tuna mousse.

'It is an art all too seldom met with,' Adam declared, 'the correct slicing of cucumber. In Victorian times there was – I believe – an implement or device for the purpose.'

'I just used a sharp knife,' Emma said.

Tom had stayed silent, remembering the foolish way he had quoted Leigh Hunt to Emma when she had been picking roses for the flower festival. Adam had, as usual, outdone him.

'In Greece cucumber is cut in chunks, thick chunks,' said Daphne. 'It makes a lovely salad, with tomatoes and *plenty* of oil.' She cast about in her memory for the Greek word for this particular salad, failed to remember it, but then decided that nobody would have been interested anyway.

'Greek food is *not* one of my favourites,' said Adam, smiling. 'One would hardly go to Greece for the cuisine – just as one wouldn't go to some churches for the music. A beautiful country, of course,' he smiled again as if at some private joke, 'but *not* a treasury of gastronomic memories.'

'Well, no, that isn't what you'd go to Greece for, as you said,' Tom agreed. The sight of the mousse – the 'shape' – in its flowered dish had brought a memory of another kind, the picture of Emma as he had seen her some months ago now, holding that same dish in her hands as she stood in the window when he passed by.

Still on the same subject, Adam now invited them to guess where he had once enjoyed 'a most memorable sole nantua'.

His hearers were not familiar with the most celebrated fish restaurants, so there were no informed guesses. Only Beatrix ventured to suggest that it must have been somewhere in France at some unexpected place, perhaps a shabby little bistro or quayside café, with oilcloth on the tables, the sort of place where lorry drivers went.

'The décor was unpretentious, certainly,' Adam said, 'you'd hardly expect it to be otherwise – in a clergy house.' He turned to Tom. 'I don't know whether you ever visited Oswald Thames and his set-up at St Luke's? They had a quite remarkable housekeeper in those days.'

'I knew about St Luke's, of course,' said Tom, rather stiffly, 'though I never went to the clergy house.'

'This housekeeper was a man – Wilf Bason – and by no means a good plain cook,' Adam smiled, obviously remembering another private joke. 'I was only a fledgling curate then, but my tastes were already formed.'

'Sole nantua,' said Isobel, firmly bringing the conversation back to the point. 'That's a sauce, is it?'

'Yes, made with crayfish,' Adam explained. 'You would poach about a dozen small crayfish in a *court-bouillon* with white wine and herbs.'

'Mortlock and his friends caught crayfish in Somerset,' said Tom but nobody took up the reference, Adam remarking that the flavour of Somerset crayfish would hardly be up to a nantua sauce.

Emma served the next course and poured Liebfraumilch, hoping that Adam would refrain from comment on the wine and the possible origin of its name. She now wished she had not invited him, not having realised how he would monopolise the conversation. Even when the subject of food was abandoned, Adam turned to her with a coy reference to her 'visitor', the gentleman who had been seen with her at the flower festival.

Beatrix shot a quick glance at her daughter on hearing this, but the subject was not developed. Emma brushed it off with the information that he had been 'only an anthropologist', somebody she had known for a long time, as if this could dispose of any romantic possibilities.

'No doubt he was studying village life and the interaction of its inhabitants in a festival situation,' said Adam sarcastically. 'One knows the kind of thing.'

'It's such a pity to bring that kind of thing into the country,' said Isobel obscurely. 'There's so much else to be studied − history, for example' − here she glanced hopefully at Tom, who instinctively drew back − 'and *natural* history, wild life. I always love a walk in the woods.'

'We must remember that,' said Adam gallantly.

'Do you see many foxes here?' Isobel asked.

'Oh yes − and you can find their traces in the woods,' said Daphne eagerly. 'Did you know that a fox's dung is grey and pointed at both ends?'

Nobody did know and there was a brief silence. It seemed difficult to follow such a stunning piece of information.

'How fascinating!' said Adam at last. 'That's something I did *not* know. I must look out for it when I next take a walk in the woods.'

'Do you often?' Tom asked, for it was difficult to imagine.

'When the spirit moves me – and in my job one must take exercise.'

'Well, next time you do you might keep a look-out for the remains of the deserted medieval village,' said Tom. 'Heaps of stones, even the foundations of buildings.'

'Oh, I prefer to let the past remain hidden,' said Adam, laughing. 'No good can come of all this delving.'

'I'm not sure that I agree with you,' said Beatrix, and Isobel now remembered that the last time she was in the woods she *had* noticed a scattering of stones at some point. Could Tom explain what might be the possible significance of that?

'Somebody has evidently been scattering stones,' said Adam. He was bored by local history and despised Tom's researches into the subject. The short and simple annals of the poor were, in his opinion, of minimal interest – those boring and limited occupations listed in the census returns where practically everybody was an agricultural labourer.

'I'm going to get a dog,' Daphne said suddenly. 'They're so clever the way they can nose out things.'

'Even the remains of a deserted medieval village?' Emma asked.

'They do train dogs to detect drugs, don't they?' said Daphne, on the defensive. 'I have heard that.'

'Yes, man's best friend has his uses,' Adam agreed.

'Shall we move from the table for our coffee?' Emma suggested. If they were going to talk about dogs it might be as well to have a change of scene, but at least the conversation had moved away from Adam's coy references to Emma's visitor. It was not until the guests had gone home and Emma was washing up with her mother – Isobel having gone to bed – that the subject was brought up again.

'So Graham Pettifer was here,' Beatrix said. The flat statement, an oblique reference rather than a direct question, was her usual way of extracting information, Emma knew. She admitted that Graham had indeed been here and added, 'He's been here twice, as a matter of fact.'

Beatrix pondered this without comment. She knew better than to press Emma farther. During the silence some plates were dried and put away, then Emma said, 'He's having trouble with Claudia – I suppose that's why he came here.' She was *not* going to reveal that she had written to him after seeing him on television. After all, her mother had known Claudia as a student.

'Of course, he has been in Africa,' said Beatrix, 'at one of those new universities – at least they seem new to us. I can't imagine that Claudia would much care for *that*. You never met her, did you?' Beatrix smiled, remembering Claudia at college. 'A pretty, frivolous young woman.' It had been after Emma's brief affair with Graham that he had married Claudia Jenks, such a complete contrast to Emma that it might almost have been on the rebound, except that Beatrix knew it hadn't been that. In some ways – and here she must have been influenced by her studies of the Victorian novel – Beatrix felt that it would be more 'satisfactory' if Emma got married now. On the whole people tended not to marry in these days, but Emma was getting past the age for that and there was danger of her settling down into an old-fashioned spinster. Danger? Remembering other spinsters of her acquaintance – Isobel, Miss Lee and Miss Grundy, to name only three – 'danger' seemed perhaps not the right word. Yet Beatrix did not like to think of herself as a conventional match-making mother, and despised herself for asking Emma, 'And where do you come in?'

Emma hesitated, remembering the night of the flower festival and the non-event it had been. She knew what her mother was driving at but did not feel inclined to tell her the full story of that afternoon and evening – Graham's appearance in the church (perhaps she might mention that) but not the tea and the boiled eggs, especially not the boiled eggs, nor his wanting to stay the night, not because he particularly wanted to be with her but because he had left it rather late to go back and was feeling tired.

'I suppose he wanted someone to talk to,' she said.

'He stayed the night here?'

'Yes, but we slept in separate rooms. He made no attempt at anything else – rather humiliating!' Emma felt she had to make a joke of it.

'And of course a night in a cottage can't really be compared with those aristocratic Edwardian house-parties with their sophisticated arrangement of bedrooms,' Beatrix said.

'Hardly!' Emma laughed. 'And he hadn't even

brought pyjamas and toothbrush with him – ridiculous, really.'

'Well, in a way, that's what it is, isn't it, the relationship between men and women.'

Beatrix's short experience of the married state had hardly given her the right to pronounce in this way, Emma felt, nor did she believe that her mother really held this unromantic view of the relationship between the sexes – her studies of Victorian fiction would seem to indicate otherwise. It was only that she didn't want to seem too eager for Emma to enter into a 'meaningful relationship' with Graham that she adopted this attitude. All the same, there was a good deal in what she said.

'He admired the Golden Lily bedcover – I suppose that was something.'

'Will he come again, do you think?'

'I don't know – he didn't say. I suppose it depends on various things.' Emma wasn't even sure whether she wanted him to. 'What did you think of *this* evening?' she asked her mother. 'Quite a success, wasn't it?'

Beatrix agreed but found herself thinking that Emma could have made herself look more attractive. She was getting a little too old for the modish drabness and wispyness so fashionable today. Surely a dress of a prettier colour and some attempt at a hair style, either curled or neatly cut and set, might have made the evening even more successful? It wasn't as if Emma had ever produced anything that could justify such high-minded dowdiness – here Beatrix considered various contemporary women of distinction – no novel or volume of poetry or collection of paintings, only a few unreadable anthropological papers. Was she not capable of better things?

In bed that night Beatrix employed her favourite remedy for sleeplessness, going over in her mind her college contemporaries and recalling their Christian names and their appearance as it had been forty years ago. Starting with Isobel — Isobel Merriman Mound — who had looked then very much as she looked now, she moved on to the more exotically named of her fellow students. Ilse Benedikta Roelofsen, the Dane, and Alessandra Simonetta Bianco, the Italian, were two that came to mind, pictured in a college group of the time but now difficult to recall because they never came back to the annual reunion. A detailed memory, irrelevant in the way such memories often are, came to Beatrix of Ilse's hand with its red-varnished nails, surely some of the first ever seen, and Miss Birkinshaw's look of horror at the sight. Ilse would have done it to shock, but girls in those days did take more trouble with their appearance than they seemed to now. Even she and Isobel, plain and hard-working, had been neat and tidy, with waved hair and timid attempts at make-up. And, after all, she, Beatrix, had married, as anyone could learn from the college register. 'm.1939, Dudley George Howick', and 'one d., Emma, born 1940'. Dudley had been a contemporary, also reading English, and Beatrix had known him for several years before they married in September 1939. Had it not been for the war, they might never have married, but it was the sort of thing people were doing at that time, and Beatrix had always felt that a woman should marry or at least have some kind of relationship with a man. Dudley had been killed at Dunkirk, all those years ago, and since then there had been nothing much in that direction. A young, academically inclined widow with a child, as she had been, was not immediately attractive or accessible, and then there had been her work, the Victorian fiction. Charlotte M. Yonge's novels contained more than one attractive young widow....

But Emma was a different proposition altogether – what was to be done with *her*? Nothing, of course. One did not 'do' anything about daughters of Emma's age in the nineteen seventies. This Graham Pettifer – nothing there, obviously, and the village was most unlikely to provide anybody suitable. Adam Prince, with his 'memorable sole nantua'? One couldn't help smiling here – *not* a marrying man. And poor Tom could hardly be described as an eligible widower.... Beatrix was becoming sleepy now, perhaps the thought of Tom had induced drowsiness. 'Ineffectual' was the word that sprang to mind when she thought of Tom – not even capable of locating the site of that ridiculous deserted medieval village in the woods, the D.M.V. And not all that efficient in the running of his church, either. Beatrix found herself remembering certain lapses of detail (presumably during some temporary absence of Miss Lee) – Christmas decorations still up on the first Sunday after Epiphany, daffodils on the altar at Quinquagesima – surely incorrect? – which Tom ought to have picked up but probably hadn't even noticed. But of course he had lost his wife, one must remember that, and was saddled with the unfortunate Daphne. Poor Tom, and poor Daphne – definitely poor Daphne.... Beatrix slept.

*

Tom was so much nicer than Adam Prince, Emma thought, going over the supper party in her mind as she lay waiting for sleep. He was an essentially good person. As well as preaching about heaven he had also given them a sermon about helping one's neighbour, and she was sure that he meant it. But to get down to practical details or brass tacks, could Tom *really* help her if she asked him? Would he, for example, be capable of cleaning her top windows, which was what she really needed?

Isobel fell asleep quickly and dreamed that she was walking in a bluebell wood with Adam Prince – highly unsuitable! She woke in the middle of the night, thinking of Shelley's poem,

> I dream'd that, as I wander'd by the way,
> Bare Winter suddenly was changed to Spring....

All those flowers – violets, daisies, 'faint oxlips', wild roses and others she couldn't remember (no fox's dung there!), and the gathering of a nosegay of all these and then the last line, much loved and quoted in her girlhood,

> That I might there present it! Oh! to Whom?

Like Beatrix she too went back to college days, a memory of that time coming to her, but of somebody not at all like Adam Prince.

13

There was a good summer that year. The mud in the lanes dried into hard ruts and the fields were burnt and bleached like an Italian or Greek landscape.

Martin Shrubsole nodded his approval when he saw his mother-in-law setting out for a walk in the woods with Miss Lee and Miss Grundy. He was unaware that the main purpose of the walk was to catch a glimpse of Sir Miles and his guests at the manor — mother was taking exercise, that was the main thing. And they had been lucky — if you could call it luck — to be rewarded by a sight of Sir Miles standing on the terrace with a group of ladies in summer dresses. By concealing themselves in a thicket, the walkers had been able to watch for some minutes while others came out from the house with glasses in their hands (it was just before lunch) and food was set out on white-painted garden tables. The sound of laughter came through the trees.

'In the old days', Miss Lee reminded them, 'people didn't eat and drink out of doors like this, though there were wonderful picnics, of course. Miss Vereker was a *great* one for picnics.'

'Miss Vereker...?' Magdalen Raven had forgotten for the moment who Miss Vereker was.

'The girls' governess,' Miss Grundy said. As if anyone could fail to know about Miss Vereker the way Olive was always going on about her!

'Oh yes, I remember now. I suppose she didn't live in this cottage?'

They had left the thicket and were passing the cottage in the woods which looked attractive in the hot weather, shaded by a grove of trees.

'No, one of the keepers lived here, but now they prefer a council house.'

'It would be such a romantic setting for a young couple, wouldn't it?' said Miss Grundy. 'I suppose Sir Miles could let it.'

'Oh yes, it's certainly habitable,' said Miss Lee. 'Miss Vereker might have preferred it to West Kensington, where she now lives, but of course she didn't have the chance.'

'My daughter feels it ought to be offered to some homeless family,' said Magdalen, 'though it would hardly be suitable, one feels. Remember in the war how the evacuees hated the country?'

'One fears the elemental forces of Nature,' said Miss Grundy.

Her companions seemed unable to comment on this and the conversation moved into more comfortable channels. It was time to be getting back for their own lunches – perhaps a salad eaten out of doors, inspired by the example of Sir Miles and his guests. It would certainly be hot in Greece and no doubt Daphne would be eating at a taverna – wasn't that the word? As for Tom, they had noticed him mooning about in the churchyard that morning – things did get rather out of hand when Daphne was away.

*

There was hay round the gravestones – the grass in the churchyard was badly in need of cutting, Tom realised. They had discussed it at the last meeting of the parochial church council. And was there no way of restraining or controlling the excesses of the village mourners? Could nothing be done to educate their execrable taste? Christabel Gellibrand had suggested at that same meeting that elaborate curb-stones, green marble chips and florid gilt lettering disfigured the general appearance of the churchyard. Some graves even had vases of artificial flowers on them, surely a disgrace in a rural area? Were there not rules that could be applied and enforced by the rector? Here several meaningful glances had been directed towards Tom, but he had just smiled, admitting that of course there *were* certain rules, but who was he to attempt to apply them, to act in what would undoubtedly seem a high-handed and unfeeling manner towards fellow human beings at a time of sadness, still suffering the grief of bereavement? After all, everybody couldn't be blessed with the gift of good taste (like Christabel G.). It was difficult to answer this, unpalatable, as it was to acknowledge a common humanity with those who would cover their graves with green marble chips or even, in one instance, a sickly piece of statuary which had somehow got itself put up in the fifties (before Tom's time as rector).

But in the far corner under the yew trees the sugary seventeenth-century cherubs, the newness of their faces blunted with the years, glowered at him over their tantalisingly indecipherable inscriptions. Perhaps even they had once been new and in deplorable taste? It was too late now to do anything about the churchyard, bolting the stable door and all that – the place was already spoilt. Only the older graves and the mausoleum, with its chaste granite obelisk, were likely to please the few who noticed such things.

Even though the interior of the mausoleum was not to Tom's taste, there was something attractive about the idea of chilly marble on a hot summer day, and he pushed aside the velvet curtain and went in.

'Ah, rector....'

Tom had not expected a greeting and was startled when he saw that Dr G. was already inside the mausoleum. Tom had sometimes wondered why Dr G. should, like himself, have a key to the mausoleum. Its inhabitants were surely beyond his help now.

There was something slightly ridiculous about the two men confronting each other in this way and in such a place, and after the doctor's first, 'Ah, rector...' and Tom's response of, 'Well, Dr G....' they stood smiling at each other, Tom's hand resting, almost in blessing, on a cool marble head, and the doctor appearing to be examing the contours of a marble limb as if he were probing for signs of a fracture.

What are *you* doing here? Tom wanted to ask, and yet in a sense both had an equal right to be here, though neither could expect to end their days in the mausoleum. But it was Dr G. who put the question to Tom, turning the tables in an unexpected way. 'What are *you* doing here?' he asked. 'I never expect to find anybody else in this place.'

'Do you come here often?' The trite social enquiry was out before Tom realised it.

'Oh yes, I come here quite often.' The doctor's tone was casual.

'There's a young man who comes to see to things,' Tom said. 'I met him here one day.'

'Yes — an arrangement was made — to see that the place was kept decently and in order. One does feel that's how it should be kept.'

Almost as if it concerned him personally, Tom thought, irritated by the doctor's attitude. As if he owned the place — but of course this was an absurd reaction, for why shouldn't the doctor have as much right to enter the mausoleum as anybody else? In fact more right, because he had been so long in the village and could even remember the last survivors of the de Tankerville family.

'Did you ever know...?' Tom began, indicating the marble representations surrounding them.

'Well, hardly *these*. The girls, certainly, and Miss Vereker — she was fond of coming here.'

'Miss Vereker?' Tom was at a loss.

'The last governess.'

'Of course!' Tom's thoughts had gone back to the seventeenth century, where he recalled no such name. 'Miss Vereker, the last governess — how sad that sounds. She taught the girls at the manor?'

'Yes, she was quite a young woman in those days.'

'And she liked to come here? A strange taste in a young woman.'

'Well, she had the interests of the family very much at heart. She used to put flowers here at Easter and other times.... I was just taking a stroll through the churchyard and thought I'd look in — funny that we should meet here,' said the doctor, now more genial, 'but after all, you and I are rather in the same line of business, aren't we?'

106

'Yes, I suppose we are,' said Tom, but whereas the doctor's surgery was full, the rector's study was empty – never any queue there. So there *was* a difference. Yet there might be a means of getting together and in a rather useful and practical way, for it now occurred to Tom that he might ask Dr G. to give a talk at one of the winter meetings of the history society. 'Death in the Olden Days' or words to that effect? He was sure the doctor would be able to think of a suitable subject.

Of course Dr G. said he would be delighted and the two men left the mausoleum, each feeling satisfied as if it *had* been a social occasion. So his 'Do you come here often?' wasn't so out of place after all, Tom thought.

Going back to what he thought of as his solitary lunch – and, indeed, with Daphne away it was a solitary meal – he happened to glance down the village street and see Emma going into her cottage, holding a letter – or it might have been a postcard – in her hand. Had she not seemed to be preoccupied with whatever news the communication contained, he might have suggested a drink at the pub. At least this was what he imagined himself doing – in practice he would probably have said nothing and so missed his opportunity. Still, tomorrow was another day – the day of the history society's summer excursion, and it promised to be at least a fine day. The clergy nowadays seldom included the weather in their prayers, but there were other blessings to be hoped for as well as sunshine.

14

Tom knew in advance that the party joining in the history society's summer excursion would consist mainly of middle-aged and elderly women from neighbouring villages − 'Tom's history ladies', as Daphne called them. Mary, Janet, Leila, Damaris, Ailsa, Myrtle and Hester − he knew them all by their Christian names, and they were undoubtedly the backbone of the society. And of course there were also a few from his own village − Miss Lee and Miss Grundy (whom he did not call 'Olive' and 'Flavia'), Dr Shrubsole's wife Avice and her mother (Magdalen?) and lastly, as he had hoped, Emma Howick, no doubt in her role as anthropologist and student of village life. One or two of the original village inhabitants also came along, not as local historians, for they cared little for such matters, but 'for the ride'. Among these was Mrs Dyer, determined to have her share of anything that was going, and almost as if to humour the rector in his childish obsession with the old days and people being buried in wool.

The only man in the party, not counting Tom, was Adam Prince, wearing jeans (a more successful buy than the pair he had given to the jumble sale).

'Your sister need hardly have gone all that way for sunshine,' he said to Tom.

'Oh, but Daphne goes to Greece for much more than that,' said Tom. 'And she really needs to get away.'

'Yes, we all need to get away, perhaps women especially,' said Adam. No doubt he was remembering women who had worked for him in the days when he was a parish priest, for he smiled mysteriously and Tom wondered if he was about to embark on one of his reminiscences of his former life. But his next remark was about the weather – they were really lucky to have such a beautiful day.

'I only hope we can find a shady spot for tea,' said Mrs Dyer, 'or we shall all get sunstroke.'

'Unlikely, Mrs Dyer, in our temperate climate,' Adam assured her.

Tom was less confident but he remembered that there were some fine trees in the grounds of Seedihead Park, where they were going, and hoped they could eat their tea underneath them.

Mrs Dyer went on to tell them all about a 'mystery tour', taken by the old people's association of a neighbouring village (the Evergreen Oldsters), on just such a hot afternoon as this on which they were now setting out. One of the old people on the journey home had been observed to be curiously silent, not joining in the sing-song.

'And do you know what?' Mrs Dyer waited for an answer.

'He was dead?' said Emma brightly. 'Or was it an old woman?'

'No, it was an old gentleman.'

'I thought as much – a woman would have more consideration than to do a thing like that, to die on an outing, with all the inconvenience.'

'Oh come, Miss Howick – aren't you being a bit hard on us?' Adam protested.

'He was sat in his seat,' Mrs Dyer went on, feeling that attention was being diverted from her, 'quiet, with his mouth open – they thought he was asleep.'

'But he was dead,' Emma repeated.

'They didn't know what to do – should they stop the coach or go on?'

'And those notices you see outside pubs – NO COACHES or COACHES WELCOME,' said Emma, embroidering the theme. 'Which to stop at? That must have been a problem.'

'It would seem best in those circumstances to return home,' said Adam. 'Did they do that?'

Mrs Dyer seemed flustered by a direct question and began to protest that it was in another village and how should she know what they had done.

'I expect they stopped the sing-song,' said Adam, 'when they saw what had happened. Or perhaps history doesn't relate that detail.'

'No – one wonders what we are failing to record now that future historians will blame us for,' said Tom. 'It's impossible to cover everything.' He recalled that several members of the society were going round the villages with tape-recorders in an attempt to capture the 'immediacy' of local happenings as they occurred, but the results so far had been curiously disappointing. They lacked the vividness of à Wood or Aubrey or Hearne, he felt. Perhaps we were all flattened out into a kind of uniform dullness these days – something to do with the welfare state and the rise of the consumer society. And then we were taken care of from the cradle to the grave, weren't we, and that must have an effect....

The coach drew up at a handsome gateway flanked by stone animals of an indeterminate species – lions, their features blunted by age, or some mythical beast. The driver said a word to the lodge-keeper and the coach proceeded to move slowly up the drive. This was shaded on either side by thickets of trees, but the surface was broken and uneven. The owner had only recently opened his park and house to the public.

'You'd think they'd make a better road,' said Mrs Dyer as the coach lurched along. 'Is this where we have our packed tea?' She peered suspiciously into the dark woods on either side.

'Plenty of shade here, Mrs Dyer,' said Tom cheerfully. He stood up in the back of the coach, a feeling of liberation coming over him. He knew from experience of such occasions that not everyone would wish to accompany him on a conducted tour of the house – some would prefer to walk in the grounds or sit down under the trees. He looked forward to a congenial talk with Emma and was pleased when he saw that she was waiting to go round the house, waiting almost meekly, like a school-girl in her blue and white cotton dress.

Emma's appearance of meekness concealed a preoccupation with the letter she had received yesterday from Graham Pettifer and the strange news it contained. He wrote of his desire to 'get away from things', to have a chance to 'get down to' the book he was working on. He didn't say anything about wanting to see *her* again, yet the amazing revelation at the end of the letter did seem to indicate a desire for her company, if nothing more, for he then said quite casually, 'I'll be spending the rest of the summer in a cottage I'm renting in your district – thought I ought to warn you!' The way he had

111

put it was ambiguous, and after the flatness of the flower festival evening she was at a loss to predict what their future relationship might be. And where was this cottage he was going to rent – why had he not asked *her* to find something for him? The only cottage she could think of was the one in the woods – could it possibly be that?

'Have you got a freezer, Miss Howick?' The voice of Magdalen Raven broke in on Emma's thoughts. It seemed irrelevant when they were examining the Jacobean embroidery on a pair of curtains, but no more so than Emma's speculations about Graham Pettifer.

'I? A freezer? No, I haven't.'

'Mummy, she probably wouldn't have, living alone,' said Avice impatiently. 'Just that little compartment at the top of the fridge, like you had, remember? You can keep things up to three months and it's quite useful, but no good for us, of course. We need the very biggest one, what with meat and the veg and fruit from the garden, and I always make an extra casserole, and cakes and bread....'

'Really?' said Emma politely. 'Even bread?'

'Oh yes – there's really nothing you can't freeze, or almost nothing. Cucumber isn't very successful....'

'There *is* a connection with the Civil War,' now Tom's voice was breaking in. 'We shall be shown the room where certain of the Royalists are said to have met....

'Are said to?' Adam repeated. 'Don't they know?'

'One hesitates to claim that kind of knowledge,' said Tom, 'but the tradition has been handed down – there is a room at the top of the house known as the king's room.'

'That does seem to indicate something,' said Emma. 'Could Charles himself have been here?'

The rest of the party had moved on and Emma found herself alone with Tom at the foot of a narrow staircase.

'That person who was with you at the flower festival,' he said suddenly, as if wanting to put the question before anyone else joined them, 'was that a relative?'

'A relative....' Emma found herself wanting to laugh – 'relative' was the term anthropologists used in their dry accounts of 'social organisation'. 'You mean Graham Pettifer? I used to know him when I worked in London.'

'Ah, London. I expect you got to know a lot of people in your work there.'

'Yes, I did, certainly. I used to go to a centre for anthropological studies and often met colleagues there.'

'Colleagues....' Tom considered the word.

'People in the same line of business – as you might meet other clergy or people interested in local history.'

Tom looked very doubtful at this but said nothing.

'Then one often met people in libraries.'

'Ah, libraries,' Tom said, but his face clouded over, as if while acknowledging the use and value of libraries he was remembering his sister's friend Heather Blenkinsop and her unnatural interest in the problems of hedge-dating.

The silence induced by the thought of libraries was broken into by Miss Lee and Magdalen Raven, obviously in a state of agitation.

'It's Miss Grundy – something rather upsetting – she's had a kind of turn....'

'It must be the heat,' said Tom. 'I was rather afraid something like this might happen. I blame myself,' he added. It was so much easier to take the blame, almost expected of him.

'Oh, it's not *that*,' said Miss Lee impatiently, 'not *that*

113

kind of turn – more like an *experience* – she says she's *seen* something, some person from the past.'

'A ghost?' Emma suggested. 'Or something like Miss Moberly and Miss Jourdain at Versailles?'

'We'd better go to her,' said Tom, 'see if there's anything we can do.'

They found Miss Grundy in a small anteroom, sitting on a folding chair, surrounded by a group of sympathetic but puzzled fellow tourists. A white-haired woman, wearing a flowered nylon overall, was standing over her holding a cup of tea.

'One of the housekeepers,' Magdalen whispered, 'she's been so kind.'

Would tea be the most appropriate drink in the circumstances? Emma wondered. But it was what everybody would think of, what would spring to mind.

'What did she see?' Tom asked of whoever was prepared to answer, for Miss Grundy seemed incapable of speech but sat staring in front of her.

'A young man with long hair, wearing a brightly coloured coat – rather in an Oriental style, she said, when she told us – she was a bit confused, of course, and now she doesn't seem to want to say any more,' said Magdalen. 'Perhaps Avice would know what to do – but she's gone on ahead.'

'There's no need to bother your daughter,' said Miss Lee, irritated by the fuss. 'It was probably a modern young man she saw – you know how young people dress now and how long they wear their hair. Come along, Flavia,' she said firmly, 'we're going to have *our* tea now.'

'Yes, tea would obviously be a solution,' said Tom to Emma.

The little episode had created a bond of sympathy

between them and both seemed conscious of it. Tom reflected on the difficulties of living with a person with whom one did not always see eye to eye. Emma had the same kind of thoughts and then found herself wondering about Tom and Daphne and speculating on why he hadn't managed to achieve a more congenial living arrangement or 'life style'. Surely he, an attractive and intelligent man, could have contrived to marry again?

Some members of the party had already established themselves under a tree on the lawn, not in the dank woods they had seen on entering the park. Emma observed that Mrs Dyer and her companions were sitting at a little distance away from Tom and the history ladies who were crowding round him, but she was sure it was none of Tom's doing. No doubt he would strenuously attempt to maintain equality however uncomfortable it might be – it would be Mrs Dyer who would separate herself and then blame him for it.

Adam Prince lowered himself carefully on to the ground – his new jeans were still a little stiff.

'I hope you won't judge our efforts by the standards you expect in your restaurants,' said Miss Lee, handing him tea in a green plastic cup but not caring in the least what his opinion was. Adam Prince's 'work' was a joke in the village – it seemed hardly credible that people could be paid money to go around eating meals at expensive restaurants.

'I'm sure the tea will be up to your usual standard,' said Adam, now the smooth-tongued clergyman rather than the restaurant inspector; after all, he had a long experience of the more humble side of catering.

'Can we picnic in the grounds of our own stately home?' Emma asked. 'The manor, I mean.'

'We've never tried,' said Tom. 'Somehow the question has never arisen. I think we should feel there was something inappropriate about it – too near home, perhaps.'

'In the old days', said Miss Lee, 'the school-children were given a tea in the manor grounds in August.'

'That kind of thing's not necessary now,' said Avice. 'People can stand on their own feet without patronage of that kind.'

Of course – Mother's Pride and Heinz baked beans (thanks, Mum), Emma thought. There was no need for the Lord of the Manor to entertain the children of his tenants in these days.

'But can people stand on their own feet?' Adam was asking. 'People seem less capable now – they seem to need more help rather than less.'

'Oh well, there are the supportive services, certainly,' Avice agreed, 'and that's just as it should be. But all that patronage and paternalism or whatever you like to call it has been swept away, and a good thing too.'

'Perhaps the people have been swept away too,' said her mother.

'Yes – I certainly miss the manor and all it stood for – we haven't got any kind of centre to the village now,' said Miss Lee.

'I suppose the clergy and the doctors have taken the place of the gentry,' Emma said.

Avice was prepared to acknowledge this, though she thought the doctors should have been placed first. Tom merely smiled; he was thinking of the encounter with Dr G. in the mausoleum and how we all came to the same thing in the end – dust and/or ashes, however you liked to think of it.

'Do you ever hear anything of Miss Vereker?' Tom asked Miss Lee. He had been reminded of 'the last governess' and how she had liked to visit the mausoleum.

'Yes, we keep in touch. I had a card at Christmas, a charity card, of course – was it the National Trust or the Gardeners' Benevolent Fund? I can't remember, something to do with Nature. She wrote a few words on the back.'

'I find most people tend to do that, now that the postage is all the same,' said Magdalen.

'Miss Vereker is giving up her flat and going to live with her nephew and his wife,' said Miss Grundy, speaking for the first time since her 'experience'.

'She would miss her flat,' said Magdalen. 'It's always rather sad to give up one's independence.'

'Oh Mummy, what a way to talk! You certainly haven't done that,' said Avice. 'I don't know what we should do without you – all your little jobs in the house and your baby-sitting – nobody could say *you* weren't independent.'

'I'm going to have a cigarette to keep the midges off,' said Magdalen suddenly.

'Now you know what Martin thinks about smoking,' said Avice on a warning note.

'Yes, it is agreeable to smoke out of doors sometimes,' said Adam, offering his old-fashioned silver cigarette case. 'Try one of mine, Mrs Raven.'

'Does the governess – Miss Vereker – come back here sometimes?' Tom asked. He had never heard that she did but it occurred to him that it might be possible to pick her brains, even take a tape-recording of her memories of life at the manor.

'She hasn't been lately,' said Miss Lee. 'The fare would be rather a drain on her resources, even with a Senior Citizen's rail-card.'

There was a brief silence of embarrassment. Tom wondered if the P.C.C. might do something, rector's discretion fund sort of thing, but he didn't like to suggest it.

'Better for her to stay where she is, in London,' said Miss Grundy, who was thinking of the choice of churches even in West Kensington where, she believed, the nephew and his wife lived.

'You'll be glad to have Daphne back, won't you?' said Miss Lee. She felt that Tom got somehow out of control — though she could hardly have specified in what way — when his sister was on holiday.

'She talks of getting a dog,' Tom said, imagining the animal bounding all over the place, upsetting everything.

In another bus on an equally hot day Daphne rested her eyes on the grey-green of the olive groves, miles and miles, kilometres and kilometres of them, stretching as far as one could see. She let the sound from the driver's transistor radio pour over her, loud blaring music, songs with an Oriental strain. She closed her eyes, basking in noise and heat. Now she was hearing again the croaking of the frogs as they had walked last night in the town, and in a side street catching sight of whole animals — lambs, she supposed — roasting on spits. Then, earlier, dazzled by the ugly white cube-like buildings of a village baking in the mid-day sun, such a contrast to the dull damp greyness of her home. She did not consciously compare them, living entirely in the present with no

118

memory of any kind of past. She remembered seeing animals crowded together in a kind of shelter in a field, and for some extraordinary reason this reminded her of Tom's history ladies, but only for a moment. She did not dwell on the memory but pushed it away from her.

The Sunday after the history society excursion, Emma went to Evensong. She found the ill-attended service more restful, even more 'meaningful' than the morning 'family' service with its crying children. She did not gain much from the sermon, for she was inattentive, but she had the impression that it was not one of Tom's better ones, an unsuccessful mingling of past and present. Afterwards she hurried away, not waiting to say goodnight in the porch.

Opposite the church there was a cottage which always interested her because its garden was crowded with derelict motor-cars. The owner seemed just to deposit his old car when he bought a new one, like a snake shedding its skin. The process reminded her of old animals, or even old people, being sheltered in a kind of rest-home. There was something peculiarly charming, even beautiful, about the sight of the cars, one still shrouded in the grey plastic cover which had protected it from the rain of the nineteen fifties, and Emma stood for a while looking over the broken-down wall into an orchard where through the trees she caught sight of something that looked like a bull-nosed Morris, surely a vehicle of historic importance? She wondered if Tom knew about it, but then of course his historical interests lay farther back and he probably regarded the abandoned motor-cars merely as an eyesore, as some of the villagers did. Yet it was all a sort of history and was there not something significant and appropriate about this particular kind of graveyard being opposite the church – a kind of mingling of two religious faiths, the ancient and the modern? 'A Note on the Significance of the Abandoned Motor-Car in a West Oxfordshire Village' might pin it down, she felt.

Once home she sat with her notes and forgot what she had just seen. Later she took out Graham's letter again and pondered over it. There may be an unlimited number of things that can happen to the ordinary person, but there are only a few twists to the man–woman story. For instance, it would be more satisfactory if Graham could expand on the bare information contained in his letter – if he could indicate something of his feelings, even. That might help her to clarify her own, for she was not sure whether she wanted him or not. There is such a thing as the telephone, she thought, glancing at the silent instrument. Its fashionable shade of grey suggested peace and repose, (unless one thought of grey as the colour of desolation, which it might also be).

When the telephone did ring she was not surprised to hear Graham's voice and to learn that the cottage he was renting *was* the cottage in the woods, 'the ruined cottage', as it was called. Apparently, however, it was habitable, but did the milkman deliver there? Perhaps Emma could find out? And bread, potatoes and a few basic groceries – he was sure Emma could arrange that?

15

Tom did not go away for a summer holiday that year,
even when Daphne returned from Greece. He was
relieved that she did not yet show any sign of getting a
dog – perhaps the prolonged heat-wave was not the
most suitable time. As for himself, the quick journey
back into the seventeenth century by time machine,
which was the sort of holiday Tom would have liked
most, was still to be invented. He did not fancy Spain,
where Mrs Dyer and her son and daughter-in-law were
going, or Miss Lee's Christian guest-house ('The
Anchorage') in the West Country, or even Miss
Grundy's few days in London, visiting congenial
churches. The middle summer months were not the
best for festivals and Tom felt he had long since grown
out of that particular kind of self-indulgent
churchgoing. The Shrubsoles were to take a cottage in
Cornwall, where Avice's mother would be available to
spend long days on the beach with the children, while
Adam Prince took his ruby-red Renault over to the
Dordogne and wandered round in search of truffles and
Mombazilliac, the most refined sort of busman's
holiday. Dr G. and Christabel went to Scotland and
stayed with old friends in a castle. Tom was glad that

121

Dr G.'s clergyman brother was not coming to caretake in the house this year, for on one occasion he had been rather too eager to help out with church services and it had been embarrassing having to admit that they never had incense and possessed neither thurible nor thurifer. Robbie and Tamsin Barraclough were the most adventurous of the village holiday makers, travelling overland to the East — Afghanistan, some said, or was it India? — somewhere in that direction.

Emma was expecting her mother and Isobel to come to the cottage some time during the summer, though they planned to stay in Isobel's cottage in the Lake District in August. Why was it so eminently suitable that a headmistress should have a cottage in the Lake District? Emma wondered. Obviously something to do with Wordsworth and the Victorian love of mountains, for the cottage had belonged to Isobel's grandfather.

The week before Graham was due to arrive at the cottage he was renting, Emma had an old school-friend, Ianthe Potts, to stay with her. She always felt guilty about Ianthe, who had doggedly kept up with her since school days when Emma would have let their acquaintance drop. Ianthe worked in a museum and had for some time cherished an unrequited passion for a fellow worker. Because of this, and also because Ianthe lived in a rather dreary flat on the wrong side of Kilburn High Road, Emma felt bound to invite her for a weekend now that she was living in the country and the weather was so good.

Emma noticed that the hopelessness of her situation had now inclined Ianthe to concentrate more on her health and on preserving herself for whatever the rest of life might have in store for her. She was more impressed by there being two doctors in the village than by the tranquil charm of the honey-coloured stone buildings or the spectacular display of summer flowers in the cottage gardens. They went for several walks, including one past the cottage where Graham was soon to live. Ianthe commented on the romantic setting, though she feared it might be damp with so many trees round it.

'You once had an affair with him, didn't you?' she said, in such a way as to put whatever there had been between Graham and Emma very firmly into the past with no prospect of any future. Emma found this irritating, for although she had no strong feelings for Graham – indeed, hardly knew how she felt about him – it was not for Ianthe to imply that there was nothing between them. But she decided to let it pass. Instead she began to ask Ianthe about her own affairs; was it still Ian, was he still the one?

'I'm afraid so,' Ianthe said. 'But there's not much hope. You see, I've found out that he's gay.'

Her lugubrious tone and appearance – she was tall and droopy, with mousey hair hanging in curtains round her pale face – made Emma want to smile and even to protest at the use of this unsuitable word. But of course it was the word in current use to describe the situation. Ian – another un-gay sort of person if ever there was one – shared his flat and his life with a young man called Bruno, so that was that.

On Sunday morning they went to church.

'Your vicar's good-looking, isn't he?' Ianthe said. 'Is he a celibate?'

'No, he's a widower, and he's a rector, not a vicar.'

Emma had a good chance to think about this on the

Sunday evening, for Ianthe had to catch a train just after five ('Must be in the museum by nine-thirty Monday morning,' was her depressingly conscientious explanation), which meant that after she had taken her to the station Emma found herself going again to church and considering Tom with more detachment. He certainly *was* good-looking, but he was also 'nice', agreeable, sympathetic, however you liked to put it. Not, of course, a dynamic personality, but who wanted that? The singing of the hymn

> For the beauty of the earth,
> For the beauty of the skies,

with its lines about the joy of human love (brother, sister, parent, child), which invariably led on to the contemplation of other, more interesting kinds of love, made Emma realise that Tom needed a wife and Ianthe needed a husband. Could she perhaps bring them together? It might work, but could she not do better for him than Ianthe? He was by no means 'averse to the company of women', she thought, pleased at that way of putting it.

On this occasion Emma did stay behind to say goodnight, but she did not mention Ianthe who had just gone, nor did Tom ask after her or enquire where she was. Instead, when there was an akward pause in their conversation, Emma told him about Graham Pettifer coming to live in the cottage in the woods. 'To work on his book,' she added, as if his coming could be for any other reason.

'Oh, that will be pleasant for you,' said Tom, doing the best he could with a curiously unwelcome piece of news. 'He will be an asset to our small community,' he added in a stiff, clerical sort of way, saying the kind of thing that might be expected of him but which meant absolutely nothing, for how could an agnostic academic, and rather a bore at that, possibly add anything to the 'small community'? Emma was disappointed in him and walked home feeling that Tom and Ianthe might well deserve each other.

When the telephone rang later on it was not Graham with further domestic instructions, but her mother. There was to be the usual old students' summer evening drinks party at her college, would Emma like to come to it? When she hesitated, Beatrix told her that she believed Claudia Pettifer would be there. Wasn't Emma at least curious to see her? 'And wear something nice,' she added, just as if Emma were a school-girl, incapable of choosing suitable clothes.

16

Emma always had the feeling at these college gatherings that her mother would have been happier if she could have presented her in a more favourable light, a daughter to be proud of – married, and the mother of fine children, or even not married, but still the mother of fine children; or, failing that, somebody with an interesting career, a television 'personality', a successful actress or even a novelist – anything that distinguished her, made her stand out from the crowd drinking wine on this summer evening in the garden of a women's college. But Emma, as well as being only a very average anthropologist who had published nothing but a few articles in obscure learned journals, wasn't even looking particularly attractive or well-groomed. She was wearing one of her drab cotton dresses in a grey and black print and hadn't even had time to have her hair done. Beside her Claudia Pettifer ('a pretty, frivolous young woman' in Beatrix's description) made an ironical contrast.

Claudia was tall and elegant, a rather formidable figure in her vividly flowered flowing kaftan. Her eyes were hidden behind dark glasses and she had adopted the frizzy hairstyle fashionable at that time – unsuitable, one might have felt, for the wife of a serious academic, obviously a sign that she was 'frivolous'. Yet who could blame her, remembering how boring Graham could be? And as he married Claudia after her own brief affair with him, Emma found herself reflecting that frivolity must have been what he wanted at that time. (But was he now reverting to his natural dullness? It was better not to see it like that.)

'Red or white?' A tray with glasses of wine was being offered.

'That seems very basic, doesn't it?' said Claudia, in a light, friendly tone. 'Is the colour all we can expect to have explained to us?'

'We can see that for ourselves,' said Emma, accepting a glass of something pale.

'What year were you up?' Claudia asked.

'I wasn't here – I was at L.S.E. I did anthropology there.'

'Of course, L.S.E.! And you know, or used to know, Graham.'

'Yes, I do know him.' For some reason Emma found herself leaving it at that – that she knew Claudia's husband.

'He's taking a cottage somewhere in your neck of the woods. To finish his book, he says.' Claudia laughed, as if it couldn't possibly be true but that she hardly cared whether it was or not.

'Yes, it's in the village where I'm living at the moment – and it literally is in the woods.'

'It would be nice to know you were keeping an eye on him.'

'Well, I'll probably see him,' Emma said. The friendly, almost cosy, note of their conversation seemed wrong, as if Claudia cared so little about Graham that he wasn't worth anybody else caring about either, especially when she added that Emma would be a most suitable person to keep an eye on him because she had known Graham 'all those years ago'.

'It wasn't so *very* long ago,' said Emma, stung by the implication of age and now uncertain whether Claudia was being cosy or just catty.

'I *know* – one feels the years just slipping away, especially at this kind of gathering.' Claudia glanced round her as if in illustration at the groups of eager women reliving old times. 'Nothing that's happened since seems all that important – people come up to you and call you by your name of twenty years ago.'

And now somebody did come up to Claudia ('Why, isn't it Claudia Jenks?'), so she and Emma were separated. They had had their encounter, for what it was worth. It was more restful and certainly less demanding to be standing next to one of Beatrix's colleagues, a mathematician who, it appeared, was responsible for the garden in some way and was worried about the drought and the effect it was having on the lawns. Emma found that she did not have to make any effort to respond – she just received and accepted the worry and helped herself to another glass of the pale wine. Pale and weak though it was, it did seem to blur her senses and induce a feeling of not caring what happened. Did people ever get drunk at these college gatherings, with their predominance of women? There were a few men present, mostly husbands, and she wondered if Graham had ever attended these functions in the past, if he had waited dutifully by the rather formidable Claudia, waiting to be introduced to her contemporaries or the dons who had taught her. She would have to ask him some time, when she described this evening and her meeting with Claudia — if she ever did.

'Did you have some interesting talk?' Beatrix asked, coming up to her.

'Oh, yes — she seems a friendly sort of girl. I dare say we'd get on quite well if we ever had to. She thought I might keep an eye on Graham, by the way.'

'Well, she'd have to say something like that.'

'A kind of joking relationship between spouses,' said Emma ironically. 'She obviously finds Graham as boring as I do.'

'Surely not,' said Beatrix, wishing Emma wouldn't talk in this way. 'But I do think she's got other things on her mind at the moment. She told me she was busy moving into a new house in Islington and that must take up all her time.'

Graham had mentioned something about this and also that the house was really too big for them and inconvenient, only two rooms on each floor, but that Claudia had decided it was what she must have, so he really had no say in the matter. Perhaps the cottage in the woods had been chosen as a deliberately contrasting summer retreat from all this. And he did have a book to finish, whatever Claudia might imply.

'It looks out over the canal,' Beatrix went on. 'A fashionable district, I believe. We shall just have to see how things go on.'

We? Emma wondered, pondering on the obscurity of this last statement. It was almost as if her mother was arranging the whole thing. 'Graham is supposed to be arriving tonight,' she said. 'I shall go round to see that he's got everything he wants.'

'Are the requisites all in the toilet?' Beatrix quoted. 'So important to remember details like that, as well as tins of soup and baked beans. And I suppose you could occasionally cook something for him.'

'Carry a casserole through the woods, you mean?' said Emma. 'Yes, I suppose I could do that.'

It was the next morning before Emma could go round to see Graham, and any feeling of excitement she might have experienced the evening before had evaporated on a hot walk through the village with a slight headache and dry mouth from drinking too much of the pale weak wine.

The village street seemed empty and foreign, with dogs and cats sleeping in doorways, but Emma had the feeling that she was being observed and seen to enter the woods. Everybody would know where she was going, for it was of course common knowledge that Graham (Dr Pettifer) was renting the cottage, though what exactly he was doing was another matter. Some even thought that, being 'Dr', he was intending to set up in rivalry to Dr G. and Martin Shrubsole, but he could hardly be holding a surgery in the woods, could he, unless he was some kind of faith healer?

The cottage looked attractive, shaded by trees even if it was damp, and the agent had arranged for the garden to be tidied and the brick path weeded. There were even a few flowers out, self-seeded marigolds and acceptable weeds, but the most interesting sight was Graham, sitting out on the grass with his typewriter at a small folding table, a stack of note-books and files on the ground by his side – the perfect picture of an academic

130

working on a book in rural surroundings. There was something self-conscious, even comic, about him and Emma found herself smiling with more than a normal welcoming smile.

He looked up at her approach and her 'Hullo – so you got here all right' was returned cordially enough, but then he said, 'I didn't expect you till later on – don't you usually work in the mornings?'

'Sometimes, but I thought I'd see if you'd settled in all right, got your milk and the groceries from the shop.' Did I once love this man? Emma asked herself, feeling that perhaps they should have kissed or at least greeted each other a little more warmly.

'Yes, thank you – the milk came this morning and I found the box of groceries – rather an odd selection.'

'Odd? In what way? I just asked them to put in some necessities, bread and butter and cheese and various tins, to tide you over.'

Graham smiled. 'I just thought it seemed odd to have tinned vegetables in the country – I'd imagined produce from people's gardens, even yours. And I don't *much* care for spaghetti hoops.'

'I don't grow vegetables,' said Emma, feeling nettled (surely that was the appropriate word?). 'You'll probably be glad of a tin of peas or carrots one of these days. As for the spaghetti hoops, I suppose Mrs Bland at the shop thought they'd do for a light supper dish.'

'We obviously have different ideas about supper. Oh, and there was a loaf of *sliced* bread.'

'You sound just like Adam Prince with your criticisms.'

'I was hoping you'd come last night – bring

something you'd cooked yourself. I've got a good collection of suitable wines inside.'

This at least showed a more personal interest and for a moment Emma imagined a future evening occasion with something she had cooked for him and a bottle of wine that went with it. And Graham and herself recapturing whatever there had been between them in the days of their first meeting at L.S.E.

But now he was working and seemed disinclined to be interrupted. 'I must work in the mornings,' he said. 'I really do have to finish this book.'

'Of course – that's why you came here, to get peace and quiet to finish your book. But why don't you come and have supper with me this evening?'

The rather formal invitation was extended and accepted, then Emma left, not quite sure whether to feel pleased or not. She had purposely not mentioned her meeting and conversation with Claudia – that would keep for another time. As she walked through the village she remembered that Daphne Dagnall was now back from Greece and that she would be giving a talk to the W.I. on her 'experiences' that evening. Emma had rather wanted to hear that and regretted having invited Graham to supper, but she could not go back again and put him off.

Noticing Tom in the rectory garden, she wondered if he would call on Graham, whether out of curiosity or as a pastoral duty. She was still remembering his foolish remark about Graham being an asset to their small community. Let him find out for himself just how wrong he had been to say a thing like that.

17

It didn't seem so bad in the village during the long summer months; even the rectory was warmer and the draughty, paraffin-smelling rooms of the winter seemed pleasantly cool and airy. Also, the realisation that there was a limit to her days here, that the time was running out, made it easier for Daphne to bear what had for so long been an intolerable burden. She and Heather had talked so much about future arrangements and now everything was nearly complete – Heather would be giving up her flat and soon Daphne must break the news to Tom that she was going to leave him. Of course the idea of 'leaving' him could hardly be compared with the breaking up of a marriage, a husband or wife leaving a spouse, but she and Tom had been together for a long time now, ever since she had 'made a home' for him when Laura died. So it would be a shock to him, a blow even, the breaking of her news.

She chose a morning when she was making pastry in the kitchen. She had just put a gooseberry tart into the oven and was wondering what to do with the bit of pastry left over, forming it into various shapes, flowers or animals and then – significantly – miniature human figures that reminded her of the little Cycladic idols she had seen in the museum in Athens. Tom was in the kitchen with her, standing idly by the table as he so often did. Now was the moment to speak.

'Tom,' she began, 'I'll be leaving here soon.'

'What, another holiday? But you've only just come back!' He adopted his usual teasing manner that she found so irritating.

'No, not another holiday. Heather has been making the arrangements – things are pretty well settled.'

'Ah, the Greek island cottage, the pad in the Peloponnese, or is it a flat overlooking the Acropolis?' He still refused to be serious.

'No, none of those,' said Daphne firmly. 'Heather has bought a house and I'm going to share it with her.'

'A *house*? Good heavens, has she come into money or something? A house in Greece would cost rather more than you had in mind, wouldn't it? Unless it's one of those ruined mansions on the way down to Tsangarada – but I can't quite see you and Heather in one of those.'

'It's not in Greece,' said Daphne patiently. 'It's on the outskirts of Birmingham, a very nice part, and I'm perfectly serious about it.'

'*Birmingham?*' Tom burst out laughing. 'What is it about Birmingham – a place one has no high hopes of, or something like that? You must be joking.'

'It's a very nice house in a very nice road,' Daphne repeated defiantly.

'But what about this dog you were going to get? You wouldn't want to have a dog in Birmingham.'

'Why ever not? Lots of people in Birmingham have dogs – there's a common and woods very near where we'll be living.'

'But not like the woods here – no foxes' dung, grey and pointed at both ends.'

'There probably *are* foxes there too – they mostly live in suburban districts now – one hears of them scavenging in dustbins – Nature is always changing.'

'When will you go?' Tom asked, thinking to indulge her in what still seemed a fantastic dream to him.

'Next week,' said Daphne promptly. 'We thought summer was a good time to move in and get settled. Heather's retiring from the library, you know. In fact, she's already left – she was having her retirement tea-party yesterday.'

'I suppose she wouldn't like to come and live here?' Tom asked. 'There's plenty of room. She could have a flat in the attics. I'm sure we could rig up cooking arrangements – you can get quite handy little paraffin cookers, I believe, or even a primus – and she could share the bathroom. She'd bring her own furniture, of course. I expect she's got furniture, as she's had a flat all this time....'

Daphne did not deign to comment on Tom's ridiculous musings but merely repeated that she expected to leave next .week. She had already done most of her packing, sorting out her few bits and pieces.

'Will you be taking any furniture?' Tom asked.

'Of course not – it's yours, isn't it? Yours and Laura's.'

'Is it? I can't remember, but if there's anything you *do* want, your bed, perhaps....'

'My *bed*? Why should I want that?'

'Well, people do usually like their own bed, especially older people. It's sometimes difficult to get used to a different bed.'

'I never heard anything so ridiculous – when you think what I've slept on abroad!' Daphne slapped the lump of pastry together, Cycladic idols and all. She could make some jam tarts which might do for one of Tom's future meals. How was he going to manage? she wondered dispassionately. He probably wasn't going to miss her at all, except in small domestic matters, would be relieved when she had gone. All these years wasted, making a home for somebody who hardly even noticed that she was there! Heather always said it had been a mistake, this rushing to make a home for Tom when Laura died. If it hadn't been for her doing this, Tom might have married again, probably would have done, seeing the way women went after the clergy. Had she protected him from a grisly fate or stood in the way of his happiness? She would never know.

'Jam tarts,' said Tom. 'Are those for tea?'

'If you like – but would you want two lots of pastry in one day, if we have the gooseberry tart for lunch?'

'Oh, I don't see why not. I'll have forgotten by tea-time. Have you told Mrs Dyer what you're doing?'

A shadow appeared to cross Daphne's face. Breaking the news to Mrs Dyer was an unpleasant task she had been putting off, telling herself that obviously Tom must be told first. 'I shall tell her tomorrow,' she said. 'No point in doing it before. I don't want it all over the village yet.'

'It will probably be that already,' said Tom mildly. 'Of course I shan't try to stop you.'

'I should hope not!' Daphne laughed. 'You could hardly stop me, could you?'

'No. I hope you'll be very happy,' he added in a formal tone, as if she were getting married. 'You and

Heather. After all, you've known each other a long time and had all those holidays together....' But sooner you than me, he added to himself.

Perhaps he had been selfish, expecting Daphne to stay here all these years when she could have been leading her own life. But he hadn't expected her to do any such thing — she had suddenly appeared, in that bewildering time after Laura's death, and now, just as suddenly, she was going away. As yet he could hardly grasp what this change was going to mean to him. At least there'll be no dog here, was his first irrelevant thought. Then he decided that he would go into the church or even spend some time in the mausoleum, meditating on the end of all things, though there was always the danger of meeting Dr G. there and he was not in the mood for that kind of encounter this morning. So in the end he retired to his study and sat among his historical records. He had sometimes attempted to keep a diary himself, the kind of record of his daily life that could rival famous clerical diarists of the past, a nineteen-seventies Woodforde or Kilvert. What was he to write about the events of this morning? 'My sister Daphne made a gooseberry tart and told me that she was going to live on the outskirts of Birmingham'? Could that possibly be of interest to readers of the next century?

18

There was something obscurely humiliating about
going into town on the bus, Emma felt, beginning with
her not knowing what the fare was and having to
fumble for the right coins when she entered. It was not
the first time she had travelled in this way, but fares had
gone up since then – 'You can't get far for twenty-five
p. these days,' as Mrs Dyer remarked, appearing to
enjoy Emma's confusion when she saw her offering the
old fare.

Tom and the students of local history really ought to
come here with their tape-recorders, Emma felt, for
there was sometimes a rich feast of village talk, the kind
of thing that might well be of interest to future
generations. But of course it would be too embarrassing
for Tom to travel on the local bus. It was moderately
embarrassing for her, apart from her ignorance of the
fare, starting off with Mrs Dyer's opening remark, 'Not
got your car today, Miss Howick?'

'No, it's being serviced.'

For some reason this seemed to amuse Mrs Dyer and
the woman sitting next to her. Emma wondered if her
words had suggested some activity of deep rural

significance, her thoughts dwelling briefly on cows and bulls, but she preferred not to speculate.

Nor was Mrs Dyer's next question any less embarrassing.

'How's that friend of yours getting on in Keeper's Lodge?' she asked. 'He's lucky to have you taking food to him.'

This was of course a reference to Emma having been seen taking a casserole to Graham one evening. She was not sure who had seen her — even though the casserole was half concealed in a basket she had been conscious of its awkward presence — but of course Mrs Dyer had got to hear about it. 'Carrying a casserole through the woods' — how ridiculous that sounded! Emma could not help smiling, but before she could answer Mrs Dyer's query the bus had stopped at the far end of the village and a woman she had met at Miss Lee's coffee morning got in. Emma seized on her gratefully, reminding her that they had met before and also remembering that her name was Mrs Furse and that she was the woman who didn't drink but had no objection to others drinking. And for her raffle prize she had preferred a mirror hideously decorated with bar-bola work to the bottle of wine given by Adam Prince.

Mrs Furse sat down opposite Emma, Mrs Dyer and her crony starting a conversation of their own. But Emma could hear that they were discussing the same subject that Mrs Furse now began to introduce, in a hushed tone.

'What will he *do*, the rector, now that....'

Emma pretended not to grasp immediately what Mrs Furse was talking about, though she knew quite well what it was. Some obscure desire to protect Tom from

139

the village gossip and speculation had come over her in a strange way, so that Mrs Furse was obliged to spell it out, 'His sister going off like that.'

'She didn't exactly go off.'

'Well no, not go off in *that* way. But she *has* gone, hasn't she? Left the rectory?'

'Oh yes, she has,' Emma admitted. A car had been seen taking Daphne off, to the station, some thought, with 'quite a lot of luggage'.

They had now reached the next bus stop and a few more people got in. At the same time Tom could be seen approaching from the opposite direction in his old Mini traveller.

'Goodness!' Mrs Furse seemed suitably awestruck, as when people say 'Talk of the devil!' or as if the sight of a person risen from the dead had been granted to them. 'I didn't expect to see him driving about.'

'I suppose he has to carry on as usual,' Emma said. 'Visiting people in the village, and after all this isn't the only church he's responsible for.'

'All this history he's always going on about,' said Mrs Furse with unexpected bitterness. 'That's more likely what he's doing.'

Searching for traces of the deserted medieval village in a motor-car? Emma asked herself, but kept her thought to herself.

'What about his food? And would he be able to do his own shopping?'

'Oh, I don't think he's all that helpless,' said Emma. 'Men in these days do seem better able to cope.' All the same she did rather doubt Tom's ability — surely she wouldn't find herself carrying a casserole to the rectory?

'And he'll have Mrs Dyer,' said Mrs Furse.

'Oh yes,' said Emma, conscious of Mrs Dyer's presence behind her. She seemed to be talking about Tom too – 'that savoury rice, you just add water and boil it up' must surely refer to some dish she had left for him.

'Perhaps *we* ought to do something about it, or the parochial church council,' Mrs Furse went on. 'The ladies, that is. I'm surprised Miss Lee hasn't done something.'

'He could have meals with Mr Prince,' said Emma, suddenly struck by this brilliant idea. What could be more suitable – even if totally inappropriate – than the two men getting together in this way?

This idea had also occurred to Tom, but more as a joke as he remembered Adam's *spaghetti al dente* (how many minutes' cooking was that?) and his habit of 'surprising' himself in his wine cellar.

The day after Daphne left Tom had strolled into the pub, not so much to have a drink – he was not the type of rector who mingled easily with the village people, even in pursuit of local history – as to have a word with Mr Spears, the landlord, who supervised the cutting of the churchyard grass. For some time now the cow-parsley round the graves had been over and given place to what could only be described as hay. Something must obviously be done about it.

'Good morning,' Tom said.

'Morning, rector.'

'About time the grass was cut again,' Tom said, in what he hoped was a pleasant, easy tone of voice. He had been practising how he would put it on his way to the pub. He had ordered a half of lager, aware that it was probably regarded as a 'ladies' drink', and sat down in a corner. Then he had brought out his remark about the grass, but there was no answer. He had forgotten that Mr Spears was sometimes a little deaf. He took a sip of lager and tried again. 'I was wondering about that grass,' he said more loudly.

'A wonderful thing, grass,' said Mr Spears. 'Reminds me of that hymn.'

The old lines came back to Tom,

> Within the churchyard, side by side,
> Are many long low graves;
> And some have stones set over them,
> On some the green grass waves.

Presumably that was the hymn he meant, not one they ever sang now; 'morbid', whether classed with hymns 'For the Young', as it was in A. and M., or anywhere else. Tom couldn't remember whether it had been included in the English Hymnal, he thought probably not; it had some questionable lines....

Mr Spears was saying something further about grass, either that he had intended to cut it but had no scythe, or that he hadn't been able to get round to doing anything about it yet. Tom's diversion into Mrs Alexander's hymn had caused him to miss the main point of what was being said, and at that moment there was another diversion. Adam Prince came into the bar.

'Sorry to hear about your sister,' he began. 'I gather she's deserted you and gone off to Greece.'

'Not Greece,' said Tom. He was tired of having to explain about Birmingham, with the inevitable jokes.

'But you have a competent housekeeper?' Adam

142

asked, as if he had no idea of the rectory set-up.

'Only Mrs Dyer for rough, as they call it, though she does occasionally leave me something I can heat up.'

'You know what you should do,' Adam said. He was always very free with advice as to what one should do, Tom felt, and generally it was the kind of advice it was impossible to take seriously, but on this occasion it might be worth listening to what he had to say.

'You should....' Adam paused to throw some instructions to Mr Spears concerning the pink gin he had ordered. He was teaching him how to concoct this drink, with just the right suspicion of bitters so that it didn't look like a glass of *vin rosé*, as when he had first made it. 'You should enlist the help of the ladies.'

Tom smiled. 'But how on earth? They all *know* Daphne's gone. What more can I do? Put a note in the parish magazine?' He was joking.

'Exactly! It must soon be time for your monthly letter. When do you "go to press", as we so grandly put it?'

'Early next week. I ought to be getting the stuff together now.'

And then, just as he had instructed Mr Spears in the concocting of a pink gin, so now Adam began to instruct Tom in the concocting of a suitable letter for the magazine to, as he put it, 'touch the hearts of the ladies'. It wasn't at all the kind of letter Tom would have written himself: he would never have thrown himself on anyone's mercy, let alone that of the women of his congregation, or used a phrase like 'kind hearts and culinary skills', but in the end he had to allow that there might be something in the idea. Perhaps he *ought* to mention Daphne's leaving and the problems – hardly

143

perhaps 'problems', 'changes' might be a better way of putting it – that her going had created at the rectory. And of course he must be careful not to offend Mrs Dyer, that was something else to be considered.

So the letter that finally appeared in print, and that Emma saw when she opened her copy of the magazine, read as follows:

As most of you will know by now, my sister has left the rectory to share a home with her friend Miss Blenkinsop, whom many of you will have met on her frequent visits here. They will be living on the outskirts of Birmingham, near a delightful wooded common where they will be able to exercise their dog. I know my sister will always take a keen interest in everything that goes on in the parish and she and Miss Blenkinsop will be frequent visitors to the rectory. But – and here is the big 'But' – her departure means that I shall be living alone at the rectory, coping as best I can, always with the willing and able assistance of Mrs Dyer. And I may very well have to try my hand at cooking an evening meal sometimes! It is often said that the best chefs are men, but I cannot claim to belong to that noble and skilled fraternity, so I am going to throw myself on the mercy of the ladies and put my trust in their kind hearts and culinary skills. I am asking you to take pity on me and invite me to an occasional meal in your homes, to share in whatever you are having yourselves, a simple family meal, eaten in congenial company....

Here the most interesting part of the letter ended and Emma did not bother to read any more. Why must his sister and her friend be sharing a 'home' rather than a house or cottage? Presumably Tom thought 'home', with all it stood for, would be more acceptable to his readers, just as his request to be invited to their 'homes' was also stressed. The reference to 'a delightful wooded common' also made her smile. As for the suggestion that he might be invited to share 'a simple family meal', one could imagine the dismay if Tom dropped in unexpectedly or the anxious preparations that would precede this simple family meal if it was known that he was coming. Poor Tom, whatever he did he couldn't win. No doubt he would receive a few invitations, but in the end he would be thrown back on his own resources, the packet of savoury rice, the ever-useful fish fingers or the miniature steak and kidney pie heated up in its little dish. Otherwise there might be the occasional meal with Adam Prince and herself carrying a casserole across the road. But she couldn't cope with Tom *and* Graham and didn't see herself offering any practical help to Tom. It was a mistaken and old-fashioned concept, the helplessness of men, the kind that could only flourish in a village years behind the times. Yet she couldn't help feeling sorry for Tom, pitying him even, and once you started on those lines there was no knowing what it might lead to.

19

Walking through the woods to the cottage, Emma decided that she couldn't always be carrying food to Graham. Sometimes he would have to be content with her company only, her conversation, and whatever else he might be prepared to ask and she to give. With this in mind, she had decided to wear a new dress, in colours possibly more becoming to her than her usual drab greys and browns. For it was impossible not to remember her meeting with Claudia and the contrast between them. So she had chosen a dress with a flowery pattern in shades of blue and green, in a more youthful and fashionable style than she usually wore. She did not feel entirely happy in it, especially when she met Adam Prince on her way and he greeted her almost with the equivalent of a wolf-whistle. She hoped that Graham wouldn't think she had made a special effort because she was coming to see him, but realised that there was no way of disillusioning him if this was what he was determined to think.

When she came up to the cottage, however, and saw that he was in the front garden reading a newspaper (it looked like *The Guardian*), it was obvious that something had caught and held his attention and that

146

he was not in a mood to notice what she was wearing. When he looked up from the paper and saw her all he said was, 'Did *you* know Esther Clovis had died?'

'Miss Clovis, dead? No, I certainly didn't know. Is it there? Has somebody written about her?'

'Yes, a rather fulsome bit.'

Emma sat down on the grass beside him, conscious of a shared ritual silence, a meditation on the passing of a formidable female power in the anthropological world of their youth. Esther Clovis, with her tweed suits and dog-like hair, was no more.

'Of course there'll be a memorial service,' Graham said. 'I'll get Claudia to go.'

Could one make this kind of use of one's estranged wife? Emma wondered, but did not comment. 'I suppose I might go,' she said. 'Miss Clovis did help to get me a grant once. But won't you go yourself?' She had not mentioned meeting Claudia and now the moment seemed to have passed.

'I can't spare the time – just look at all this.' Graham indicated a stack of folders and an untidy bundle of typescript.

Emma bowed her head. She ought to have noticed. 'How's the book going?' she asked, conscious of a somewhat naïve approach.

'It isn't exactly *going*,' he said, 'so you see I can't be popping up to London for all and sundry.'

'You'd hardly call Miss Clovis "all and sundry".'

'Well, you know what I mean. Anyway, that was the whole point of my coming here and taking this cottage – so that I could get on with my book. You're looking very fetching today,' he said, suddenly noticing her. 'New dress?'

'Newish', said Emma. She was not particularly pleased to be described as 'fetching' and, remembering Adam Prince's reaction, perhaps the dress had not been a good idea after all. She must remember to explain to her mother when she reverted to her old drab servant's morning-dress cotton. '*I'm* thinking of writing a book – about this village,' she said, to change the subject, 'making a kind of survey. There's quite a lot to be observed, more, really, than in my new-town study.'

'That sort of thing has been done,' said Graham in an idle, uninterested tone, coming to sit beside her on the grass. 'Do people pass along this way? Will anybody see us?' He started to kiss and fondle her in a rather abstracted way. Emma found herself remembering Miss Lickerish and the goings-on in the ruined cottage during the war. 'I hope we should have some warning,' she said, 'see them coming through the trees.'

'This is rather pleasant, isn't it?' he said. 'I feel I deserve a break from my work,' he added, as if being with her could be no more than that.

Adam Prince, taking an afternoon stroll (strictly for his health, he was not fond of walking), came up to the cottage and saw Graham and Emma 'canoodling', as he put it, on the grass. The sight filled him with distaste. One would not have expected this sort of behaviour from Miss Howick, though it was obvious now why she had appeared in a new dress. An upsetting sight in the woods was how he thought of it as he turned back and went home to solace himself with a cup of Lapsang.

Emma's old grey cotton dress was eminently suitable

148

for Miss Clovis's memorial service, and as the hot weather had broken she was wearing a raincoat, another appropriate garment which, unknown to Emma, had been the uniform of the male anthropologist of the fifties. She spent the time before the service looking round to see if there was anyone she knew rather than admiring the austere beauty of the eighteenth-century church. She recognised Professor Digby Fox, who was to give the address, with his wife Deirdre, old Dr Apfelbaum, rather bent now but still as cantankerous as ever, and a gaunt white-haired woman (could it be Miss Clovis's friend Gertrude Lydgate?) sitting with an elderly clergyman. Various others, less distinguishable in the crowd, were obviously feeling the need to honour Esther Clovis in death as they had feared her in life. But where was Claudia Pettifer? Emma had so far been unable to find her, but she had a further opportunity to look around her when she was listening to the address, only half hearing what Digby Fox was saying – how you might think that this elegantly formal setting was not what Esther would have chosen, but that it was in another sense appropriate as typifying the high standard she expected and demanded from all those whose work she was called upon to sponsor ... few would forget her advice to young researchers about to enter on a period of field-work, the comments that must often have seemed harsh, as was her criticism of written work that fell short of the high standard she demanded.... Here Digby seemed to falter, to repeat himself and stammer nervously, as if he expected Miss Clovis to be looking over his shoulder at the address he had prepared or to be listening somewhere up above. Emma felt sorry for him but as he floundered her attention wandered, and she saw that Claudia was sitting almost directly opposite her, at the end of a row. She was wearing a black coat of a silky material, a small close-fitting hat concealing her frizzy hair, and dark glasses.

'One thing we can be sure would have pleased her,' Digby continued, 'and that was the manner of her going — suddenly, you could almost say brusquely, reminding us of her own manner, that sense of bringing something to an end which, in her opinion, had gone on long enough....'

Here the address did end. The congregation stood up and sang 'He who would valiant be', their voices rising in thankfulness and relief.

It might be possible to speak to Claudia on the way out, Emma thought. Would she remember that they had met at the college wine-party? She was standing alone, perhaps waiting for somebody, and when Emma went up to her the blank gaze of the dark glasses was disconcerting, but she persevered.

'We met at that summer wine-party,' Emma reminded her.

'Of course! Red or white on the sunburnt lawn. Rather different from today.'

It was raining heavily and the two women put up umbrellas. Then, to Emma's surprise, Claudia took her arm and hurried her away from the church and into a side street where there were several small restaurants.

'Would you have a drink with me or a bite of lunch?' she asked. 'It must *be* lunch-time now. Shall we go in here?' She almost pushed Emma into a doorway where a smiling Greek was waiting to show them to a table. 'I hope you can bear Greek food,'

Claudia said. 'I just had to get in somewhere and this seemed the nearest place.'

'You saw somebody you didn't want to meet?'

'That's *right*! I spotted him in the church – you really did me a good turn, coming up to me like that. Sherry? I don't think it's a day for ouzo, somehow. Did you know Esther Clovis? I was *sent* to the service by my husband.' She made a face and took off her dark glasses – it must have been almost impossible to see anything in the dim light of the restaurant – and smiled at Emma in an almost conspiratorial way. 'This weather makes my hair go all frizzy,' she said, taking off her hat. 'I mean even more frizzy than usual.'

So the fashionable hairstyle was natural – her hair really was like that. Emma had not been prepared for this friendly approach, but perhaps Claudia was like that with everyone and did not regard Emma as a person to be treated differently. Was it reassuring or humiliating? She hardly knew, for, in spite of their dalliance on the grass, weren't she and Graham no more than 'just good friends'?

'Shall we have moussaka or do you like those little meat balls or kebab or something?' Claudia was saying.

Emma was reminded of Daphne, perhaps even now preparing a Greek meal on the outskirts of Birmingham or picnicking on the 'delightful wooded common' (though not on a day like this), and found herself smiling. 'Our rector's sister goes to Greece every year,' she said, as if in explanation, 'but now she's living with a friend near Birmingham.'

'Birmingham,' Claudia repeated. 'Graham was once offered a job in Birmingham. Should we have a glass of wine?'

Emma was not surprised that Claudia appeared to make little of her conversational opening. Mention of 'our rector's sister' would be enough to put anyone off. But Birmingham had obviously struck a chord somewhere and she began to wonder if Claudia was the kind of woman who would turn everything into some personal reference.

The food arrived – moussaka ('safer', perhaps) – with a glass of red wine.

'Dear old Digby Fox,' said Claudia, beginning to eat, 'not exactly an inspired address.'

'I suppose he said what most people felt about her,' said Emma. 'Miss Clovis *was* rather terrifying, I always thought.'

'That must have been in the days when you and Graham were at L.S.E,' said Claudia in an easy tone. 'How's he getting on in the cottage?'

'Oh fine, I think,' said Emma, as if she didn't really know. 'I've been to see him once or twice.'

'Should we have a pudding? I don't suppose there's much to choose from – vanilla ice-cream or tinned fruit and custard, that's usually the kind of thing. Or "baklava" – shall we risk the baklava?'

'Nothing more for me, thank you,' said Emma. It was disconcerting that Claudia appeared more interested in what pudding she was going to eat than in Emma's possible relationship with her husband.

'What *is* the baklava?' Claudia asked the hovering waiter.

'Very nice,' he said unhelpfully.

Claudia peered around her to see if anyone else was having it. In the end she decided to give it a try but when it was brought she began to regret it. 'It looks

152

exactly like the moussaka,' she complained. 'Don't you think so? It probably *is* the moussaka, with a different filling. This has been *rather* a mistake,' she said, in a jolly all-girls-together sort of way. 'How wise you were not to have anything else! *Are* you wise – generally, I mean?'

Emma had the feeling that Claudia wouldn't wait for her answer even if she was prepared to give it – she was only making conversation, hardly interested in whether Emma was 'wise' or not. After a pause Emma said, 'I haven't married, so you can draw your own conclusions,' but Claudia wasn't really interested in Emma's unmarried state either and immediately turned the conversation to fit her own experience. 'I sometimes think *I* married too young,' she said. 'It would have been better to have started off on a career and *then* married.... I suppose it's easier to go shares,' she added, studying the bill. 'After all, we did have the same.'

You had the baklava and I didn't, Emma felt like saying, but of course they ended up by a scrupulous division of the bill and the working out of an appropriate tip.

It was still raining when they stood in the doorway with their umbrellas. It appeared that they were going in opposite directions, so they separated with polite mutual murmurings. It had been 'so nice', this unexpected meeting. Emma realised that she had done Claudia a good turn in helping her to avoid somebody she didn't want to see, but she herself had gained very little from the encounter. But had she really imagined that they would be able to have a serious talk about Graham?

153

It was not until she had gone too far along the street to turn back that Emma realised that, possibly in the stress of some obscure emotion, she must have taken Claudia's umbrella in mistake for her own. And it was an umbrella of inferior quality. She wondered what the possible significance of that could be.

20

'Hunger lunch, did you say?' Martin Shrubsole was addressing his mother-in-law. 'Today, is it?'

'Yes, at Miss Lee's house, where I went for that coffee morning,' said Magdalen. 'I'm looking forward to the lunch – she always does things so nicely.'

'Well, I hope not *too* nicely today,' said Martin in a pleasant, even tone, only very slightly reproachful. 'After all, it *is* supposed to be in aid of the starving people of the Third World, isn't it?'

'Yes, of course, but it will be just home-made bread and cheese, fruit and coffee – a very simple meal.'

'One of my favourite lunches,' said Martin smoothly. 'A good deal more than they'll be having in some parts of Africa or India.'

'Oh Martin, we've got to eat *something*,' said Avice, who was also going to the lunch. Martin did not always feel so strongly about the Third World and was obviously going on like this for her mother's benefit. 'And we do pay for it.'

'Yes, we put money in a bowl,' Magdalen explained. 'Miss Lee has to take her expenses out of it – that's only fair.'

'You really ought to have a mush of beans or rice

and drink water,' Martin went on boringly, but Avice pointed out that you probably wouldn't be able to get the right sort of beans.

When they got to Miss Lee's cottage, however, the lunch was not quite as delicious as usual. For some unspecified reason she had been unable to bake her own bread and a shop-bought white sliced loaf was provided, certainly unlike anything that would have been eaten by the starving peoples of the Third World, yet the nastiness of its soft, moist, cotton-wool-textured slices was in some way curiously appropriate.

The bread was taken without comment, and then somebody asked if there was any news of Daphne — had she settled down well in her new house with her friend?

'We must hope so,' said Miss Lee. 'I suppose we shouldn't know if she hadn't.

'Miss Blenkinsop is rather bossy, isn't she?' said Avice. 'She'd want to have things her own way.'

'But Daphne is the kind of person who'd give in to her,' said Miss Grundy, obviously speaking from personal experience of a similar situation. 'It makes life so much easier.'

'But at least she'll be able to stand on her own feet,' said Avice. 'She did need to be independent, get away from the rectory.'

'Living with the rector in that big house — it might not have been all she'd hoped for from life,' said Magdalen, feeling that as a newcomer she was justified in offering a general comment on the position. 'Of course, I don't really know the circumstances — but what will he *do*, the rector, now that she's gone?'

'Well, he's coming here to this lunch, so that's one

meal settled,' said Miss Lee. 'Only a hunger lunch, I know, but that's one less for him to think about.'

'That letter in the parish magazine,' said Magdalen. 'I wonder if anyone....'

At this moment Tom entered the room, followed by Emma and 'that man living in the cottage in the woods'.

'*Two* men,' Avice murmured to her mother. 'We could have persuaded Martin to come if we'd known. Good heavens,' she exclaimed, for now Dr G. and his wife Christabel came in, turning what had promised to be the usual gathering of village women into something of a social occasion. The senior doctor, the rector, the academic stranger....

'Martin not here?' Dr G. asked Avice.

'No. He has his ante-natal clinic this afternoon and I always feel he needs a good lunch before that, so I've left him a casserole in the oven.'

'Christabel thought it would do me no harm to have a hunger lunch,' Dr G. said. 'How are you managing without your sister?' he asked Tom.

'Quite well, thank you,' said Tom. 'People have been so kind,' he added mechanically, feeling that he ought to say this even if they hadn't been. There had not as yet been any response to his plea in the parish magazine.

'I suppose it's not really so different for *you* to eat this kind of thing,' said Dr G. conversationally, 'bread and cheese for lunch. We pay for it, don't we?' he asked, rather too loudly. 'Put something in the kitty?'

'There's a bowl by the door,' said Miss Lee in a lower tone. 'We usually make a charge of twenty-five pence which covers expenses and leaves something over for the good cause.'

'Twenty-five pence?' said the old doctor. 'That would be five bob in proper money, wouldn't it? That seems a bit steep for a slice of pappy bread and a sliver of mousetrap.'

'It's not supposed to be a proper meal,' Christabel said sharply. 'And you'll be having your dinner tonight,' she added, as if speaking to a child.

'Do you have to join in all these village activities?' Graham asked Emma. They were standing a little apart and took the opportunity to move out from the open doorway into the garden, where others were already standing or sitting with their sliced bread and mug of weak coffee.

'I don't have to,' said Emma, 'but I quite often do.' She was surprised that Graham had agreed to join her until she realised that he wanted to 'show himself' in the village, to make it clear to everyone that there was nothing hole-and-corner about his living in the woods or about his association with Emma. By the same token there had been no repetition of what Emma thought of as the 'amorous dalliance on the grass'. She found this irritating rather than upsetting – he need not be quite so circumspect – and she was also irritated by his attitude towards her meeting with Claudia and their lunch together. He had been more interested to know what they had eaten – he rather liked Greek food – than to know what they had said about him or the situation existing between the three of them. As for the umbrella incident, he seriously suggested that Emma might like him to make a special journey to Islington, taking Claudia's umbrella and bringing Emma's back with him.

'Is one allowed to have another slice of bread?' Dr

158

G.'s voice was heard demanding querulously. 'I'm *hungry*. I notice Adam Prince hasn't put in an appearance.'

'No, Mr Prince is *working*,' said Miss Lee sternly. 'He said how very sorry he was not to be able to come. He has to go round some restaurants in the Peak District – such a long journey for him.'

Tom came up to Emma and Graham. 'Are you quite comfortable in that cottage?' he asked. 'I believe it hadn't been lived in for some time.'

'Miss Vereker had always wanted to live in it,' said Miss Lee. 'She often used to say how she wished she could – she loved those woods.'

'And now she's living with her nephew and his wife in London,' said Miss Grundy. 'It doesn't seem the same, does it....'

'Like Daphne living in Birmingham when she'd always dreamed of something in Greece,' said Tom.

'Well, we can't expect to get everything we want,' said Miss Lee vigorously. 'We know that life isn't like that.'

They all looked instinctively towards Tom, as if expecting his confirmation of Miss Lee's pronouncement, but he said nothing. Why should the clergy always be expected to have some pious bromide at the ready? he thought. It was an outmoded concept.

'*I* should like another slice of bread,' said Dr G. plaintively. 'We never had these hunger lunches in the old days. Weren't the natives hungry then?'

Now they all turned towards Graham who had, after all, been in Africa. He should know the answer to that one.

'We looked after our own people out there in those

159

days,' said Miss Lee. 'That's the answer to Dr G.'s question. Things aren't the same now.'

'No, they are not,' said Dr G., 'and do you realise that in the old days, when I first came here, it was nothing unusual for patients to *walk* to the surgery from the outlying villages – there's no exercise like walking. Now they all come in their motor-cars, or if not in their own motor-cars, somebody else's. People expect to be conveyed everywhere now – even the children don't walk to school – lolling about in charabancs you see them, when a two-mile walk would do them all the good in the world....'

'I suppose it might be dangerous for children to walk, with all the traffic there is on the roads now,' said Emma mildly.

'And have you noticed', Dr G. went on, 'how every car has some slogan on it these days? Support the Teachers – Rethink Motorways – Protect Wildlife – Don't Waste Water – I could think of plenty more to the point than those.'

'I wonder what the legendary Miss Vereker would have had on her car?' Emma asked in a low voice.

Tom was the only one to hear her. 'Women didn't drive about in cars in those days,' he said. 'Sir Giles was the first to have a car here, I believe.'

'Sir Giles de Tankerville?' Emma asked.

'A friend of King Edward the Seventh,' said Miss Lee. 'Of course I never knew him personally, nor King Edward,' she added with a laugh.

'I wonder if Miss Lickerish remembers that first motor-car,' said Tom thoughtfully. 'It might be worth investigating, though her memories don't seem to go back all that far.' Her collection of photographs, which

160

she had once displayed for him, was also a disappointment, the highlight being a picture of a goose sitting up at the tea-table, of little historical interest.

Now people began to drift away, with little prospect of more stimulating conversation and nothing more to eat. Emma noticed the same home-made pottery bowl placed to receive money as at the coffee morning. She wondered if Graham would put 25p. in for her but he seemed unwilling to compromise himself even to that extent. Would it create gossip in the village if he had been seen to pay for her hunger lunch?

Tom, seeing them go off together, with much loud talk of 'getting back to work', went quietly back to the rectory feeling depressed. It was his afternoon to visit the hospital, not his favourite occupation or one in which he felt he did much good to anyone, but it was expected of him and you never knew — something might come of it. All the same, he was conscious of feeling hungry, which was just as it should be, and envious of Martin Shrubsole, who had been provided with a casserole lunch before his ante-natal clinic.

21

Emma and her mother were picking blackberries along a lane a little way out of the village, trying to avoid Mrs Dyer who had been seen approaching in the distance. Emma braced herself to meet Mrs Dyer's comments in her raucous, almost triumphant, tones, 'You won't find many *there*, Miss Howick – I've just been along that bit.'

Emma felt like pretending that she wasn't really out blackberrying at all, just taking a walk, but there was no getting away from the fact that both she and her mother were carrying various receptacles and that they must have been seen in the act of picking.

'Couldn't you imagine a Wordsworthian encounter here?' said Beatrix when Mrs Dyer had passed with her full basket. 'Meeting some interesting old person or an idiot boy or even the rector, poor Tom, or your friend Graham Pettifer?'

'Men don't go blackberrying,' said Emma. 'Children and boys, perhaps, but not grown men.'

'And Graham is busy working, no doubt.'

'Yes, he does work hard.'

There was silence as they went on searching for the blackberries, picking what Mrs Dyer had left. Beatrix had been expecting more than Emma's bare comment on Graham now that he was living in the village.

'Has Claudia been down?' she asked.

'Been down?' Emma asked in surprise. 'Not that I know of.' The cottage in the woods was not exactly the kind of place one would have 'been down' to from a house in Islington.

'You ran into her in London, you told me.'

'Yes, at Esther Clovis's memorial service. It was a terribly wet day. We had lunch together at some Greek place and I got Claudia's umbrella by mistake – one of those ludicrous things that happen sometimes, reducing everything to the level of farce.'

'Did you talk about Graham?'

'We mentioned him, of course. And she said again that I might keep an eye on him at the cottage.'

'That was somewhat ambiguous, wasn't it? Or was she being sarcastic? Does she know about you and Graham?'

'There isn't all that much to know. I don't know how I feel about him.'

'How does *he* feel about *you*?'

'Oh, we get on quite well together,' said Emma evasively, 'and, of course, we have the work experience in common....' She sounded doubtful at this and Beatrix immediately took her up on the jargon phrase 'work experience'. What exactly did she mean by that and in what way was it relevant to a state of love between two people?

'Oh *love*,' said Emma impatiently. 'I wasn't thinking about *love*.'

'In the Victorian novel', Beatrix said, 'a young woman had nothing like this. A hero could hardly share the work experience of a governess.'

'You don't think in *Villette*, perhaps? But that wasn't quite what I meant — hardly to be compared with the years at L.S.E....'

'If you made blackberry jelly you could take some to Graham, couldn't you?' said Beatrix, adopting a more practical approach. 'And I dare say Tom would be glad of a pot.'

'I can't go taking jelly to every lone man in the village,' said Emma. 'And what about Adam Prince, while you're about it? Can you see me going up to the rectory with a pot of jelly? Tom wouldn't know what to say. And talk of the devil, here he is now, wandering aimlessly along the lane, not even picking blackberries.'

Tom seemed embarrassed at meeting the two women and murmured something about spindleberries — could Emma and Beatrix distinguish their leaves or point out the exact spot where they were to be found in the autumn? Apparently it could be of historical interest, of importance in the matter of hedge-dating.

But nobody really knew what the leaves of spindleberries looked like and Tom moved on, saying that he really ought to be getting back, there were so many things he should be doing.

'Poor Tom, I expect he misses Daphne,' said Beatrix, 'although they never got on very well. Now he has no human contact at the rectory, only Mrs Dyer coming in to clean. You'll have to take pity on him.'

'I don't see what I could do,' said Emma, 'and after all, nobody likes to be pitied.'

Beatrix glanced at her daughter, startled by a certain fierceness in her tone. She wondered if Emma was pitied in the village. Judged by the harshly conventional standards of the inhabitants, she probably would be.

Tom, too – they were a pair. She smiled. Taking pity on somebody might not always be the same as that pity which is thought to be akin to love. ' "Pity is sworn servant unto love," ' she quoted. 'Do you know that?'

'Who is it? Some obscure Victorian poet?'

'No, an Elizabethan, Samuel Daniel. Minor, I suppose, but you probably know some of his sonnets....' Her voice faltered, for Emma probably did not. It was sometimes a grief to her that her daughter was not better read in English Literature, with all the comfort it could give. A few sad Hardy poems, a little Eliot, a line of Larkin seemed inadequate solace.

'We're going round the manor this evening,' Emma said, as if the mention of Tom had reminded her. 'I suppose you'll come?' She peered down into the dark glistening mound of blackberries they had just gathered and noticed a small white grub moving among them.

'I'll put some sugar on these, then we can eat them raw,' said Beatrix, who had not seen the grub. 'Yes, I'll come tonight.' Great houses, even when they had seen better days, provided an agreeable link with her literary interests.

It was the usual party going round the manor, dominated by Miss Lee, who had 'known the family' and was, as always, very ready to point out ways in which things were different from the old days. Even the books lying on a low coffee-table in one of the rooms lived in by Sir Miles and his family drew a disapproving comment from her. 'Horses, yes, one would expect that, but old Sir Hubert wouldn't have had some of this rubbish in the house,' she muttered, pointing to the latest lurid-looking paperback novel of a popular American author. 'And Miss Vereker would *never* have allowed the girls to read this kind of stuff.'

She had doubtless forgotten that such popular literature had not been available in those far-off days, but nobody bothered to remind her of this.

'One of the girls did the flowers,' she went on, 'and Miss Vereker always did the flowers in the hall.'

'Not Lady de Tankerville?' Beatrix asked.

'No, her ladyship never cared for flower arranging. And Miss Vereker had such original ideas. There was always an arrangement of wild grasses in season – dried in the winter, of course – and she had a way with fir-cones.'

'And now we come to the chapel,' said Tom in an attempt to get away from Miss Vereker and her flower arrangements, 'a fine late seventeenth-century building.'

The chapel was rather more than Sir Miles had bargained for when he bought the house or 'acquired the property', as some put it, so he had shut it up, feeling that putting it to any secular use might bring disaster on his family. It would have been convenient to turn it into a billiard-room or even a library – though none of them were great readers – or even to pull it down, but it turned out to be a 'listed building' or something of that sort, with its carving that might just possibly be Grinling Gibbons, and its floor made of a special kind of rare marble. He didn't want some retired male do-gooder or bossy elderly woman coming snooping round and threatening to 'do' something about it, getting up petitions and that kind of thing. So the chapel was kept shut up but could be visited by parties going round the house, as on this September evening, when the days were drawing in and it was nearly dark by half-past seven. The idea of being buried in woollen seemed quite attractive in the chilly gloom of the chapel, Tom thought as he reminded the party of the edict of 1678, just about the time when the chapel would have been built. Mr Swaine, the agent, who was officially conducting the party round the house, was keeping in the background, feeling that the rector knew much more than he did about the history of the place, though not quite as much as that woman Miss Lee, who seemed to know everything about the more recent past.

'In Sir Hubert's time', she was saying, 'they had family prayers in the chapel every morning and evening.'

'Is Sir Hubert buried in the mausoleum?' Emma asked, her question coming out rather too loud and clear in one of the temporary silences.

'But of course,' said Miss Lee with enthusiasm. 'You must let me show you some time.'

'And the girls, I mean the daughters, and Miss Vereker – are they also buried there?' Magdalen Raven asked eagerly.

There was a shocked silence as Miss Lee explained about the 'girls' – one killed in the Café de Paris air-raid in 1941, the other now living in the South of France, and Miss Vereker, very much alive with her nephew and his wife in West Kensington.

'Wood came here, of course,' Tom said. 'And Dr Plot found a particularly interesting stone in the grounds – that was his only comment on the house or garden....' It had borne a shape closely resembling the female pudenda, he remembered, but did not mention this.

Beatrix was inclined to encourage Tom to tell them

167

more about the seventeenth- and eighteenth-century associations of the house, but before she could continue on these lines the talk returned to trivialities and somebody asked Tom for news of his sister.

'Daphne? Oh, she seems to have settled down very well,' said Tom heartily. 'She and her friend Miss Blenkinsop – you remember, she often used to stay here – have now acquired a dog.'

'What sort of dog have they "acquired"?' Beatrix asked in a dry tone.

Tom did not seem at all sure what sort it was. 'A large one, I believe. Daphne did tell me the breed, but unfortunately I've forgotten what it was.'

'They'll be able to take it for walks on that delightful wooded common,' Emma said, and their glances met in a kind of sympathy. Perhaps she would take a pot of bramble jelly to Tom after all, if the next lot turned out well.

'Did you get many blackberries this afternoon?' Magdalen asked. 'I saw you coming back. My son-in-law likes me to get a walk every day and I nearly came out myself, then I thought it might be better to wait a day or two if many people had been picking.'

'Miss Vereker was famous for her blackberry wine,' said Miss Lee. 'Old Sir Hubert used to say that it was better than....' She paused, unable to remember the precise name of the famous French wine it had been better than. 'Chateau something or other,' she concluded. 'I don't suppose she's able to gather many blackberries in West Kensington....'

'If this carving is *not* Grinling Gibbons,' Tom was saying, 'it is certainly by one of his pupils – just look at these swags of flowers....'

But nobody was looking. The chapel was cold ('chilly') and musty with being shut up all the time. There was a chance to see some of the bedrooms and that was going to be much more interesting. Then, at the end of the evening, there was to be coffee at Miss Lee's house and they were all looking forward to that. There would be tea also for those who did not like coffee or were influenced by the popular superstition that it was supposed to keep you awake.

'As if coffee as weak as this could possibly keep anyone awake,' Emma whispered to her mother.

'A pity Graham didn't join us this evening,' Beatrix said. 'He might have had a good influence on the level of conversation.'

'Indeed, yes,' said Tom, who had come up to them. 'Dr Pettifer would have been most welcome, but of course if he's writing a book....'

'Oh, is he writing a book, your friend?' Miss Lee asked. 'What is it about?'

'Nothing very interesting, I'm afraid,' said Emma disloyally, but why should she be loyal to Graham? Yet as she spoke she seemed to catch the eye of Canon Grundy, in his silver frame on the piano, the light shining on his high clerical collar, and the sight of him gave rise to a slight feeling of shame. 'I mean, it's a rather specialist sort of book,' she added.

'Oh I see, not popular,' said Miss Lee in a comfortable tone, as if relieved that she would not have to read it.

For the second time that evening Emma found herself exchanging a sympathetic glance with Tom.

22

As the unmistakable end of summer approached – misty mornings, the first falling leaves, the days inexorably drawing in – Graham found himself coming to the conclusion that as far as Emma was concerned he had 'bitten off more than he could chew', to quote a phrase his mother sometimes used (even his academic attempts at L.S.E. had come into that category, he remembered). Yet he had not exactly bitten anything off, it had been thrust at him in the form of Emma writing to him after the TV appearance. But he need not have responded – he could have ignored her letter, pretended he had never received it, if it came to that. Why had he sent that postcard? Vanity and curiosity mixed? He was flattered that Emma should have written and curious to see what she was like now. Well, he had seen and now he knew. Their meeting had *not* been the kind of amusing romantic encounter he had imagined – certainly not romantic, hardly even amusing, though she had a kind of wry wit. It had been an 'amusing' idea to take the cottage in the woods and he had managed to do a good deal of work, made substantial progress with his book, but the village atmosphere and Emma's apparent involvement in its activities had proved surprisingly inhibiting. Really the whole thing had been Claudia's fault. None of the Emma situation would have come about if Claudia's upsetting behaviour had not coincided with the TV discussion programme and Emma's response to it. Certainly he would not now be walking with Emma in the woods on a sultry late September afternoon after an inadequate lunch.

'This is a part of the woods I haven't really explored,' she was saying. 'I've always been intrigued by the name — Sangreal Copse — what do you think the origin can be? The rector says it comes from the land having belonged to St Gabriel's college in the old days.'

'Quite possibly, I should think,' Graham said in a bored tone. He had not really wanted to go for a walk and now he felt he was childishly 'dragging his feet', another reminder of childhood days.

'I'm sorry you didn't come round the manor with us,' Emma said. 'It was an interesting evening.'

'I was trying to finish the first draft,' he said, 'and didn't want to break off.' But really it had been the prospect of the kind of conversation and company he had met at the hunger lunch that had put him off the excursion. Also, he did not want to be seen in the village as a kind of appendage or 'boy-friend' of Emma's.

'I believe people live here,' said Emma, changing the subject. 'Look, through those trees.'

A low roof came into view and then another and another, revealing a little cluster of bungalows, each with its neat box-like garage.

'How horrid!' Emma exclaimed. 'Not exactly what you'd have expected or hoped for, judging by that evocative name.'

'Well, people have got to live somewhere,' Graham said aggressively, but really, was it worth arguing the point? There was no doubt that the bungalows – one might almost call them 'dwellings' – were ugly and out of place.

'So much for my romantic ideas about Sangreal Copse,' said Emma sadly.

They walked on along a rough road which connected the bungalow dwellers with the village and then farther into the woods, where a path led through scrubby grass and mean bushy undergrowth to another low building some distance away. And suddenly there was an appalling smell. At first it was indescribable, though as they advanced closer to it Graham found himself remembering visits to his grandmother in the country and the smell of the poultry house there when he had helped to clean it out. What could it be? Neither Graham nor Emma had so far commented on the smell as if it were a kind of social embarrassment and they did not know each other well enough or were not on sufficiently intimate terms to mention it. Graham thought again of his grandmother's poultry house, but the origin of such a stench seemed unlikely here in these bleak surroundings, yet the explanation when it came was obvious and he had been right. A gaunt wooden structure came into view and the silence was broken.

'Good heavens!' he said. 'A poultry house – apparently deserted, abandoned, but the smell certainly lingers on.'

'Of course, I remember now,' Emma said. 'Daphne Dagnall once told me – Mrs Dyer's son had a broiler house somewhere up here – this must be it.'

172

'The business failed, did it?'

'I suppose so, you could imagine ... so he turned to the second-hand junk trade and now has what he calls an antique shop.' Deceased Effects Cleared, she remembered, but did not say the words out loud. It seemed curiously, even bitterly, appropriate to the walk she and Graham were now taking, to their whole relationship now fizzling out at the end of summer.

'Chickens.... Chickens seem to be associated with failure and disaster, don't they?' he remarked in an idle, making-conversation sort of way. 'In literature, I mean – those stories of unsuccessful chicken farms at the end of the First World War.'

'But this is a different sort of chicken farming. There's something not natural about it. The confinement of the birds,' she declared, and then wondered why she had used such a ridiculous phrase.

'No, of course it's different. Not free range.'

She wondered if he was remembering the boiled eggs, that time he had arrived in the church on the day of the flower festival. But no more was said on the subject of chickens or eggs as they walked on in silence away from the smell.

'Of course I'll be leaving here now,' he said. 'Now that the book's virtually finished.'

'Your stay here has been profitable then,' she said, pondering on his use of the word 'virtually'.

'Oh yes – I'm not displeased with the results.'

'The house in Islington will be ready to receive you,' she said.

'I certainly hope so! Otherwise I should have to stay here longer.'

They had made a kind of circle and were nearly back

at the cottage now. Graham asked Emma to come in for a drink. He had decided not to work this evening.

Perhaps he has decided to make love to me, she thought, but when she saw that with the bottle of Scotch he had produced four glasses she realised that she was obviously mistaken in her imaginings. She commented on the number.

'Yes, I'm expecting the Barracloughs – they're back, you know.'

'And they've been to...,' she began, but at that moment they appeared, full of their overland trip to Afghanistan and the various 'projects' it would lead to. Robbie's beard was rather longer and bushier than before, but Tamsin's frizzy hair and long bedraggled cotton skirt seemed much as usual. They started to talk academic shop with Graham, for Robbie was to take up a new appointment in the autumn and various personalities in the department where he would be working were discussed or torn to pieces, whichever seemed to be applicable. Emma began to wish she had not stayed for a drink – it would have been better to go quietly home and watch television, engage in some useful household task or even get on with her own work. How often must this kind of thought or reflection have occurred to a woman on such an occasion when, having been faced with alternative courses of action, she has obviously chosen the wrong one! For now the tedious process of making bramble jelly seemed infinitely preferable to this arid academic chat and she found herself wondering whether Graham had deliberately engineered this situation and had invited Robbie and Tamsin in because he didn't want to be alone with her.

'And how's your own work going?' Robbie asked politely, turning to Emma.

'It seems to be changing direction,' said Emma, thinking as much of the bramble jelly as of the notes she had made on the village. 'There are various other lines that could be explored.' That was certainly one way of putting it.

'I've often thought one could do a study of this village,' said Tamsin innocently. 'But I suppose it's such a well-worked field that there'd be nothing new to say.'

'Emma would find something new,' said Graham in a rather possessive way. 'Even if she had to make it up.'

'Well, one can't really do that,' said Robbie. 'After all, we're not novelists,' he added, smiling in a superior way into his beard.

Suddenly Emma felt unbearably irritated by the whole situation and got up to go.

'So soon?' Graham asked. 'Won't you even have another drink?' Then, when she refused, he got up too, with the evident intention of accompanying her through the woods. This irritated Emma even more, his formal politeness and the idea that a woman must be accompanied on a country walk in the dark. Yet she realised that had he *not* made the gesture she would have been even more annoyed. Women were not yet as equal as all that.

'Please don't bother,' she said. 'I shall be quite all right. It's not a particularly dark evening, anyway.'

'Maybe, but that's hardly the point,' said Graham uneasily.

'Somebody might leap at her out of the undergrowth,' said Robbie, secure in the knowledge that he had no obligation in the matter.

175

'Please don't disturb yourselves,' Emma repeated. 'I'll be quite all right.'

She and Graham walked down the front path of the cottage, Emma still protesting. Certainly it was not particularly dark, as there was a full moon. A lovely night for a walk, given the right circumstances, she felt, but Graham could hardly leave his guests.

At that moment a figure loomed up in the half darkness, a tall shape, approaching slowly. Emma saw that it was Tom.

'Why, it's the rector,' said Graham. 'Were you coming to call here?'

Tom seemed startled. Obviously he had not intended to call and the suggestion seemed to touch on some source of guilt, as if he was conscious of a failure in this direction. 'It hardly seemed a suitable time,' he said lamely. 'I was merely taking an evening walk in the woods.'

A kind of joke situation, Emma felt, and was on the point of suggesting that he must have been looking for the deserted medieval village. 'I'm just going home,' she said. 'Perhaps you'd be kind enough to walk back with me − just through the woods, of course.'

'With pleasure,' said Tom.

'If you would accompany Miss Howick,' said Graham formally. 'She has to get back....'

'Did you really have to get back?' Tom asked when they were alone.

'I got bored with the Barracloughs' conversation and I have to make bramble jelly.'

Tom expressed polite interest and the hope that some might be available for the next church sale. Emma did not reveal that she intended to give him a pot, for it might not be successful and it would not do to raise his hopes. 'Do you often walk in these woods?' he asked.

'Oh, sometimes – like Miss Vereker.'

Tom laughed. 'Oh, Miss Vereker. Miss Lee never tires of telling us what Miss Vereker did.'

'Will you come in for a minute?' Emma asked at her cottage door.

Tom hesitated, not because of the lateness of the hour or for any fear of scandal but because he was afraid that Emma might be going to offer him a cup of weak coffee or even tea.

'We could have a drink,' she said, wondering if tea or coffee would be expected. But she brought out a bottle of vermouth and they sat down with the bottle between them on a small table. Emma was feeling depressed, for this was not the sort of ending she had imagined for this particular evening. The blackberry juice had not yet finished dripping through its bag, so there was nothing for it but to sit down and drink with Tom, 'the rector', making whatever kind of conversation came to mind. She thought of asking about Wood's visit to the manor in sixteen seventy something, but in the end fell back on Daphne and the usual question about how she liked living in Birmingham.

A cloud seemed to come over Tom's face – people were always asking him that. 'Her friend Heather is rather bossy', he said, 'with the dog's regimen and that kind of thing. Daphne mentioned some disagreement they'd had about whether to give the animal tinned or fresh meat or something that apparently looks and tastes like fresh meat but isn't....' He frowned, adding, 'What could *that* be?' as if it were important that he should know.

Emma mentioned a substance she had seen advertised on television – dogs eating from various dishes, unable to tell the difference.

'Ah, that would be it.' Tom seemed relieved.

'Your sister shared a flat with her friend before, didn't she?'

'Yes, so she knows her failings. Heather was a librarian,' he added, as if this might explain the failings.

'I suppose she's used to making decisions, taking action – that sort of thing?'

'About a dog's diet?' said Tom, and they began to laugh. The tension and irritation, beginning with Graham and the walk in Sangreal Copse, seemed to go out of the evening.

'Sangreal Copse,' Emma said. 'An ideal setting for the end of summer, don't you think?'

Tom was inclined to go into the historical niceties of the area, and even to quote something from Wood, when Emma would have preferred an account of the decline and fall of Mrs Dyer's son's broiler house. But when she expressed a rather conventional regret about it being the end of summer, he was reminded of the brief holiday he would be taking – a few days in London, mid-week, staying with Dr G.'s brother in his clergy house – and he began to tell Emma about it.

'I shall be spending some time in the British Museum.'

'Oh yes?' Emma did not ask what he would be doing. It might be enough for him to sit in the reading room, just for the change. 'You could have stayed in one of those hotels nearby, but I suppose even those are ruinously expensive now.'

'Yes, they are. Actually it was Christabel G.'s idea

that I should stay with her brother-in-law the first time I wanted to go to London some years ago.'

'How strange! I wouldn't have expected....'

'No, you wouldn't.' Tom smiled. 'London to her is Onslow Square and Harrods, of course — though she's rather less respectful about Harrods these days — so it was quite a leap of the imagination for her to think of anyone staying in any other district. And Father G., as they call him, is very kind....'

If there was a slight hesitation in Tom's manner, a subtle lack of enthusiasm at the prospect of staying with Father G., it was only because he was remembering certain material discomforts of the clergy house, and also the danger that he might be called upon to assist at a weekday evening Mass. But, consulting the Kalendar, he had made sure that there was no likelihood of that happening in the week he had chosen — still nothing but the green vestments and all those long hot Sundays after Trinity. No Saints' Days at all.

Summer was also ending for Adam Prince, in disagreeable, even disquieting, experiences. The first, in a motorway café where, surrounded by eaters younger and less fastidious than himself, he sampled (in the course of duty) a kind of 'high tea' that was not at all to his liking. The second, in the impersonal surroundings of a motel or 'Post House', where his bodily needs were adequately catered for but there was a chilling lack of human contact. No charming elderly lady (and Adam frequently enjoyed conversations with such on his travels) knitting in the lounge after dinner; no cordial 'Buon giorno, signore' from a smiling young waiter, bearing his breakfast on a tray high on his shoulder, as nostalgically recalled in some Roman *pensione* not too far from the Spanish Steps. Adam's plastic 'continental' breakfast appeared early and mysteriously outside his door as if brought by computer, which it may well have been. That last might be a suitable note to introduce into his report which he would be writing when he got home.

But his desire for human contact, wasn't that the most disquieting thing of all? Could it be that he was getting old?

23

Even though the days were shortening, the dahlias round the mausoleum made quite a show in the late summer sunshine.

'Quite a show,' Magdalen remarked to her son-in-law as they sat at lunch, 'those dahlias round the mausoleum – such brilliant colours.'

'Were you in the churchyard this morning, mother?' Martin asked. He did not want to suggest that being in the churchyard was morbid or undesirable in any way. He had developed his own sensible approach to death, which he tried to impart to his patients and any old person with whom he came into contact. It was good to have a relaxed approach to the proximity of gravestones – perfectly O.K. to walk in the churchyard (indeed, it could often be a useful short cut to somewhere else, the pub, for example) – but was it to be encouraged, this *frequenting* of the place, walking round studying the gravestones, as his mother-in-law appeared to be doing?

'Yes, I've been there – the rector wants us to make some notes on the graves – I mean, what kind of stone is actually used, as well as reading and transcribing the inscriptions where we can. Of course it's not always possible – some of them are rather worn, the old ones, and some of the stones seem to have sunk into the ground so that you can't make anything out. You have to crouch down on all fours to get a look at them!' Magdalen laughed. 'I expect people wonder what we're doing – if anyone sees us, that is.'

'The rector expects you to do this? He expects elderly people to crouch on damp ground, just for a whim of his?' Martin seemed indignant.

'Oh, it isn't just a whim of *his* – it's for the county historical record of graveyards, and you know how keen the rector is on that.'

'Well, I think it's most unsuitable,' Martin grumbled. 'He should get some of the younger ones to do it – or even do it himself.'

'There aren't enough younger ones – and I find it interesting, getting to know who's buried where and what kind of stones they have. Some of Miss Lee's family's there, you know. Did you have a good surgery this morning, dear?'

'Well, perhaps "good" isn't the way to describe it. A busy one, certainly, as always.'

'Keeping them out of the churchyard?' said Magdalen chirpily. 'Though there's still plenty of room in the newer part. But you really ought to see those dahlias by the mausoleum, they're a picture....'

Martin got up from the table. Conversation with his mother-in-law, though no doubt therapeutic for her, was so often a waste of time for him. 'A walk in the woods or fields would do you more good than crouching in a damp graveyard,' he warned finally, 'whatever the rector may say.'

'I was wondering if we could ask him to supper one

evening,' Magdalen said. 'He seems lonely, now that his sister's gone.'

'Oh well, that's up to you and Avice,' said Martin. He couldn't concern himself with that kind of social invitation or with the minutiae of housekeeping – what was in the larder or the freezer, what would be suitable to give the rector and that kind of thing. All the same, it might not be such a bad idea to have some friendly dealings with the man, to get to know how things were going in that direction, whether he was now making plans to get himself moved into a smaller house, and if he was, whether the old rectory might be up for sale. 'Dr Martin Shrubsole, The Old Rectory' sounded a highly suitable address for a rising young physician.

Avice of course agreed with him, when it was put to her like that, and they were very soon discussing what they should have to eat.

'You remember that letter in the parish magazine?' Avice said. 'He wanted to be invited to a *simple* family meal, or words to that effect, so he won't expect anything special. But I don't suppose he gets much if he depends on Mrs Dyer, so maybe we should make a bit of an effort.' And of course she also felt that it might be advisable to feed him well and put him in a good humour in case the question of the rectory came up. But was Tom the kind of person to be influenced by food and drink? – after all, he wasn't Adam Prince – and would the future of the rectory rest with him, even if he did decide to leave it for a smaller house? Wasn't it the Church Commissioners or the Diocesan something or other that decided things like that?

'There'll be something off the joint to make up,' Avice said, 'so it could be shepherd's pie' – for, after all, he was a kind of shepherd – 'or moussaka, though I expect Daphne has given him enough of that. No, I think it had better be chicken – that seems the obvious thing.'

'And perhaps one of your nice puddings,' Magdalen suggested. 'I expect he'd like that. I don't suppose he ever gets a nice pudding.'

Tom had temporarily forgotten the parish magazine letter and the bit about the simple family meal, when he saw Martin about to carve the chicken. He was taken back to his days as a curate, when poultry was still regarded as an appropriate meat for the clergy, though in these days it seemed to be more an everyday sort of meal. Turkey was now more highly thought of – advertised on television as fare not only for Christmas but in Holy Week as the thing to get for Easter, with the grinning family pictured dining off slice after slice of the breast. Tom recalled that Mrs Dyer and her family usually had a turkey at Easter, and sometimes also at Whitsun, or the 'Spring Bank Holiday' as it now was.

'I suppose you haven't been getting so much Greek food lately,' Martin said in a joking way.

'No – Daphne's practising her art on the outskirts of Birmingham.'

'How does she like it there?' Avice asked.

Tom hesitated. 'Well, they have a dog, you know,' he replied, as if that answered the question. 'It has to be exercised every day, of course. She and her friend share in looking after it.'

'Miss Blenkinsop is a librarian, isn't she?' Magdalen asked.

'She was, but is now retired. They are two "Ladies in

Retirement".' Tom smiled. 'Wasn't there once a play of that name? Some years ago?'

Only Magdalen could remember that.

'But she was glad to leave the country, wasn't she?' Avice persisted. 'I always had the impression that she didn't really like it here.'

'Oh, I wouldn't say that,' Tom protested. 'She missed Heather, I think they'd shared a flat before she came here.'

A lesbian attachment? Martin wondered, as he had before, his card-index mind slotting it neatly into place, but perhaps it was unlikely. 'Didn't your sister want to live in Greece?' he said.

'Yes, I think she did,' Tom said, 'but that proved an impossible dream – as so many dreams are.' He paused, throwing out this rather intractable substance, almost threatening the soft to-and-fro of the conversational pat-ball. It created a moment's silence, for the others did not know quite what to do with this offering, being unwilling to learn more about Tom's impossible dreams, or even to speculate on what they might be.

'I expect you miss your sister,' Magdalen said at last, 'being by yourself in that big house.'

Tom looked surprised, for that aspect of Daphne's going had not occurred to him. It seemed a rather suburban concept, his being by himself in a big house.

'Have you ever thought of moving to somewhere smaller?' Avice asked.

'Well, no. It *is* the rectory, after all, and I suppose as rector I'm expected to live in it.'

'I believe some clergy *are* getting smaller houses, even having them specially built for them,' Avice went on. 'The wives find it so difficult to manage in these great rambling old places.'

'Really?' said Tom politely. 'That hadn't occurred to me. Having no wife I suppose I'm out of touch.'

'There are those bungalows going up opposite the church,' Martin declared.

'Oh yes – where those old cars were dumped.'

Was he being sarcastic? Martin wondered – equating himself, as rector of a country parish, with a worn-out and dumped old motor-car? But no, he was too nice a man for that, too lacking in guile. 'I can't imagine you living in one of *those*,' Martin allowed generously. 'I wasn't suggesting....'

'No – it wouldn't be altogether suitable. I have so many books and papers – I do need a bit more space. But they'd be near the church and churchyard, wouldn't they?'

'They're old people's bungalows,' Avice pointed out in her usual bossy way, 'for rehousing some of the old people in the village.'

'So you see, Martin, I should be even nearer the gravestones if I moved into one of those,' said Magdalen. 'My son-in-law has been ticking me off for spending so much time in the churchyard,' she explained to Tom.

'Oh, I'm sorry about that. Mrs Raven has done such valuable work for our survey,' said Tom. 'I do hope it isn't being too much for her.'

Martin brushed this aside with a smile and gave Tom more wine. 'What do you think of this?' he asked. 'Not too bad, in my opinion.'

'Splendid!' said Tom. He had been appreciating Martin's generous refilling of their glasses, Avice and her mother drinking very little. An excellent thing in women, this abstemiousness in wine-drinking, though it hadn't been quite what Lear or Shakespeare meant when they coined the phrase.

'Adam Prince recommended it,' Martin said. 'So I ordered a case.'

'Have you a cellar?' Tom asked.

'Unfortunately not – that's one reason why we must get a larger house – though not of course the only one.' He flung a teasing glance towards his mother-in-law.

But they did not return to the subject of the bungalows or the possibility of Tom moving to a smaller house. A hint had been given, a seed sown, the idea perhaps put into his head – there was nothing more to do for the moment but wait and see.

Appreciating Martin's admirable port, Tom reflected that the rest of his parishioners would have difficulty in living up to the hospitality he had enjoyed this evening. It was something of a relief to feel that his plea for a simple family meal with no special trouble taken had not been interpreted too literally. As he walked home, noticing the new bungalows opposite the church and smiling to himself at the idea of living in one (Anthony à Wood in a bungalow!), he found himself wondering who would be the next person to invite him to a meal. Several had murmured half invitations, obviously spurred on by conscience, and he had recently eaten scrambled eggs with Miss Lee and Miss Grundy ('Just what we have ourselves'), with the television on at a wild-life programme; also Adam Prince had invited him for next week. But there had been nothing so far from Emma, apart from the drink that evening when he had accompanied her through the woods. And of course there was Dr Pettifer, that man living in the cottage. Wouldn't he be going back somewhere soon?

187

What was there between him and Emma, anyway? Nobody seemed to know, though Mrs Dyer had hinted in her usual way. Tom hadn't listened, turned the subject, asking her if she remembered some of the old songs they had sung when she was a girl. But all Mrs Dyer could contribute was 'Run, rabbit, run' and 'We're going to hang out the washing on the Siegfried Line' from the early days of the war, and that hadn't been quite what he meant.

As Tom was arriving back at the rectory, Daphne was letting the dog out and remembering the jumble-sale picture 'Thy Servant a Dog'. But wasn't it *we* who were the servants, especially of dogs and cats, she thought as she waited for him near the bushes at the back door. It was a damp chilly evening, the kind of evening that made her wonder why she and Heather hadn't gone to live in Greece after all, fulfilling those ambitions they had once had. Or was she the only one who had had them, who still dreamed of a Greek village, even a modern Greek village with a garage and hideous square white concrete dwellings baking in the sun, and a dusty little square shaded by a single gnarled tree? That very evening they had been using the salad servers they had bought last year on a visit to the Meteora, and Heather had scolded Daphne for putting them in the water when she was washing up – the decoration on the handles might be damaged and they would never be able to get another pair. 'Oh, surely we'll go up there another time?' Daphne had protested, but now, standing waiting for the dog in the damp darkness, she began to doubt. Perhaps they would never go to the monasteries again, but surely they would go to other

188

places? Yet Heather was now talking about a cottage in Cornwall for next summer – a fellow librarian knew of one that would accommodate four and she and her friend and Heather and Daphne would make up a party – quite near Tintagel, marvellous cliffs and such seas in the rough weather! Greece had been so *very* hot last summer, and Heather's swollen ankles in Athens seemed to be the only memory she had retained of that wonderful holiday.

'Come *along*,' Daphne called impatiently to Bruce, the dog. 'Surely you've finished by now?'

In the sitting-room Heather had made a cup of tea.

'I wonder how Tom's getting on,' she said chattily. 'All the ladies of the parish flocking round him, I shouldn't wonder.'

'Yes, I expect the history society members will be looking after him,' Daphne agreed. And he would be able to 'lead his own life', whatever that might be, just as she was.

'Do *you* notice anything different about this tea?' Heather asked.

'It seems weaker?'

'Exactly – *weaker!* Different tea bags. I shan't get *those* again. Poor economy.'

24

The dahlias by the mausoleum reached a perfection of flowering when Graham Pettifer finished his book, as had been his intention, and prepared to return to London. After that the flowers would fall and die, and by the time they were blackened by the first frost Graham would be gone. The house in Islington was now ready for occupation so there was nothing to keep him in the village. It would be quite a change to return to civilisation! he said. Not that the cottage hadn't been delightful in its way, he hastened to add, but with the winter coming on he could see that such charms as it had might well turn into disadvantages, even positive discomforts. So he loaded the back of his car with clothes and books, strapped a table on to the roof-rack – the table he had imported to hold his typewriter – and was gone.

When it was time to say goodbye, he took Emma in his arms with a warmth and affection he had not shown during his time at the cottage (except when they had made love on the grass and been seen by Adam Prince), making it seem that he could hardly bear to leave her. He was so very grateful for all she had done for him – the groceries, the casseroles, even the sliced bread. And of course they would meet again soon. The three of us, Emma thought, though he had not mentioned Claudia except by implication – obviously she would be waiting in the house in Islington. He had also said something about the curtains in the room that was to be his study – could it be that the design was that same Golden Lily as the bedspread in Emma's spare room? Claudia must have chosen it.

Friendship between men and women was a fine thing, Emma thought as she stood on the brick path of the cottage garden. She had walked through the woods to take what might be a last look at the cottage and also to see whether some tomatoes she had planted in pots in the front were ripening. Peering among the leaves she saw that Graham had picked them all, even the green ones. Would Claudia be making green tomato chutney then?

She went up to the door and tried it but the key had never worked properly and it was easy to open and go in. The sitting-room looked tidy, only an old copy of *The Guardian* and an empty packet of cornflakes in the wastepaper basket, and a few tins to be disposed of in the kitchen. She sat down on a battered armchair covered in ugly red material and with the stuffing coming out. She noticed a piece of paper on the mantelpiece, a cyclostyled list of the church services for that month. Had Tom – or somebody – struggled through the woods to deliver this useless information? Or had it just been an excuse for the messenger to snoop around, in the hope of surprising 'goings on'? Emma would never know.

She got up and went upstairs to the bedroom. Nothing here. Graham was a disappointingly tidy person, but there was a book on the rickety bamboo table by the bed – a collection of seventeenth-century verse. Had he intended to leave it behind and had it any significance? The book opened not at a love poem but at one by Richard Crashaw, with the curious title 'Upon Two Green Apricots Sent to Cowley by Sir Crashaw'. She began to read it, but the wry metaphysical conceits meant nothing to her, only the uneasy suspicion that the poem might have a kind of bitter relevance to her relationship with Graham. But he would never have thought of that. No doubt he had borrowed the book from somebody and forgotten to return it....

There was a sound downstairs. Somebody had come into the cottage through the front door.

'Who's that?' Emma called out, thinking for a moment that it might be Graham coming back for any one of a number of reasons.

'Sir Miles Brambleton's agent,' came a loud confident voice. 'And what are *you* doing here? This cottage is supposed to be locked.'

'Exactly!' said Emma, revealing herself at the top of the stairs. 'And the lock is broken. It ought to have been seen to long ago. It's a wonder vandals haven't been in, now that Dr Pettifer's gone.'

'Oh, it's Miss Howick – I'm sorry....' Emma wondered at the change in the agent's tone. He sounded respectful now and she realised that it was because of her own approach, boldly tackling him about the broken lock so that she appeared in the role of a bossy caring woman, concerned about the prospect of Sir Miles's property being vandalised.

'That's all right,' said Emma graciously, 'but I do

192

think that lock ought to be seen to. One of the estate carpenters, perhaps....'

'You have to be joking!' was his less respectful reply. 'It's not like the old days now.'

'No, I suppose not. Was this cottage lived in by one of the keepers then?'

'Yes, and I believe it was a favourite walk for the young ladies and their governess.'

'Ah yes, the girls and Miss Vereker. I can imagine them coming here....'

'Will Dr Pettifer be returning?' the agent asked on a more practical note.

He will never return, she thought, but just said aloud that she didn't know and that the lock really ought to be seen to.

'Can I offer you a lift back to the village?' Mr Swaine indicated his Land Rover parked outside.

'No thank you, it will do me good to walk.' And to spend the rest of the day getting on with my 'work', Emma thought, and even, since Graham had gone and the summer was over, to contemplate the future. What was she to do now? The only practical thing that occurred to her was to do something that had been on her conscience for some time, to ask Tom to supper. But this evening, a simple family meal indeed, on the spur of the moment. After all, they were two lonely people now, and as such should get together.

She gave Tom the remains of a joint of cold lamb and potatoes in their jackets, with home-made apple chutney from Miss Lee's bring-and-buy sale. To follow there was tinned rice pudding (though Emma did not reveal that it was tinned) with some of her bramble jelly. The meal was washed down with a bottle of the same wine she had been drinking when she had seen Graham on the television programme all those months ago. At the last minute Emma had produced a small piece of cheese, but it looked so unattractive that neither of them attempted it.

Tom wanted to say that he was glad she hadn't made any special effort with the meal, and indeed it had been just the kind of thing he liked, but was afraid of seeming ungracious.

'So your friend has gone,' he said, over coffee. 'Dr Pettifer has departed,' he emended stiffly, wondering if that was a better way of putting it.

'Oh yes – he's back in London now.'

'He borrowed a book from me.'

'There *was* a book left behind – a collection of seventeenth-century verse – was that it?'

'Yes. He was here one day and wanted to check something, so I lent it to him.'

This seemed unlikely, given the kind of book Graham was writing; almost as unlikely as Graham being at the rectory. He had never mentioned it.

'He'd had a letter from his wife,' Tom explained. 'I suppose she may have quoted something.'

Remembering Claudia in the Greek restaurant, Emma wondered, but nothing was impossible in a marriage. She found herself blundering in unknown territory, with the trite reflection that communication between Graham and Claudia had not only been about the curtains for his study. And the poem probably hadn't been the one about the two green apricots, either.

'Laura was fond of that book,' Tom was saying. 'She liked the metaphysicals.'

It was the first time he had ever spoken of his wife and Emma was not quite sure how to react. It wasn't as if he was a man only lately bereaved; there could be no danger of intruding upon a recent grief. Laura had died more than ten years ago, or so it was said, and he had not married again. So perhaps she had been his first and only love?

'I expect you still miss her,' Emma said, feeling that, although it was an inadequate comment, honesty was less awkward than polite social murmurings. She was rewarded by Tom's simple matter-of-fact reply.

'I suppose I do, in a way,' he said. 'But after all, one gets used even to the state of missing somebody, and as a person she seems remote now. Sometimes I can hardly remember her.'

'What was she like?'

Tom hesitated. Perhaps he was less capable of describing what Laura had been like than of giving an account of the village in the late seventeenth century, but Emma gathered that she had been a contemporary of Tom's at Oxford, clever, amusing, 'good' socially in a way Tom never could be. It was difficult to gain any impression of her as a person or to speculate on whether one would have liked her. Perhaps she was not as nice as Tom – a sharp, clever woman married to a good man? What had she died of? What *did* people die of nowadays? Not consumption or a Victorian illness like typhoid or scarlet fever – but cancer and various kinds of heart disease were always with us, so probably it was one of those.

'She developed leukaemia,' Tom said, 'and in those days there was nothing to be done. Perhaps it might have been different now.'

And there might have been a formidable wife at the rectory, Emma thought.

'You didn't – in time, of course – think of marrying again?' she said.

'Well, Daphne came, as you know.'

Emma felt she couldn't bear another conversation about Daphne and her dog, but to her relief Tom went on talking about the time after Laura had died, and even seemed to be making excuses for not having married again.

'I didn't seem to have the chance, or meet anyone suitable....' He must have been aware how feeble he sounded. As if a man, especially one connected with the church, couldn't meet women if he had a mind to, however much hemmed in by a sister!

'But people in your parish – in London and here – there must have been....' Emma protested.

'Oh, there were, of course. Every church has plenty of women, even eligible women, but somehow.... Well, *you* haven't married either, have you?' Tom turned to Emma as if attacking her. 'Was it Dr Pettifer? Was he the one?'

Emma laughed. 'I did think so at one time, when we first met. But it didn't come to anything and then he married somebody else. I didn't see him for years until I saw him on the telly one evening and wrote to him. People go on about the harmful effect of television on children, but what about the dangers for the older viewer?'

'So that was it – your first love reappearing.'

'Well, in a way I suppose it was.'

'He must have been interesting when you first knew him.'

'How do you mean?'

'He always seemed to me rather a dull dog – on the few occasions we met.'

The idea of Graham being any sort of dog made Emma laugh again. Altogether it was turning into a rather successful evening after the unpromising start to the day. She and Tom finished the bottle of wine and the conversation turned away from Graham to more comfortable matters, one of which, rather surprisingly, concerned the mausoleum and Tom's 'worry' about it. Miss Lee had been on at him to get in touch with the people who were supposed to be looking after it. It needed to be 'serviced', just like a car, and nobody had been down to see to it for some time.

'Whatever would Miss Vereker say if she could see it now,' they both agreed.

25

When Terry Skate's little van did eventually turn up at
the mausoleum it was obvious that he was in some
kind of 'mood'. Tom feared that he probably wanted
more money or was about to announce a strike or
withdrawal of his labour in some way. That was the
usual pattern these days. Possibly he was intending to
'work to rule', whatever that might involve in the
tending of the mausoleum. But in the end it was none
of these. It was a simple but essentially fundamental
matter. The truth was that Terry Skate was disinclined
to carry on the mausoleum work because he had lost
his faith.

Tom was so surprised, even stunned, by the news
that his first reaction was one of nervous laughter, but
of course it was no laughing matter. It was obviously
his duty to go into the matter more fully, even to
attempt to restore what had been lost. When pressed
Terry admitted that there were certain aspects of the
faith that he hadn't been happy about for some time.

'Ah, you've been reading a book that's worried
you?' Tom suggested. There had certainly been a
number of books lately, he recalled, that might have
had an impact equal to that of *Honest to God* in the

early sixties, though it seemed a little unlikely that Terry would have read them.

'Oh, it's not *books*,' Terry said. 'It's those talks on the telly.'

They were standing inside the mausoleum, surrounded by the chilly marble effigies uncomfortably appropriate for such a discussion.

'I mean, university professors and that, and one of them was the reverend somebody or other. But he was wearing a green turtle-neck jumper – I *ask* you!'

The green turtle-neck jumper rather than the clerical collar seemed to have made a deep and lasting impression on Terry, who went on to complain about 'people like that' coming into your lounge through the media, throwing doubt on what you'd been taught to believe.

Tom, who had neither television-set nor lounge, was at a loss to know what to say next. Then he remembered that having doubts was no new phenomenon. We all had them at times. Adam Prince had doubted the validity of Anglican Orders, though a discussion of that question would not help Terry now. He did his best to console him, to assure him that this period of uncertainty would soon pass and that his faith would return, stronger than ever. 'After all,' he pointed out, 'much greater men than either you or I have been assailed by doubts and overcome them.'

'Oh, but that was in the old days, wasn't it? Darwin and those old Victorians.' Terry laughed, dismissing them.

There had probably been a play on the telly about that, Tom thought, coming to the conclusion that Terry wasn't really all that worried about his doubts. He was accepting them – men speaking on the box had swept away his childhood faith and he was not prepared to be reassured by Tom. There was really something in what Emma had said about the dangerous influence of television on the older viewer. The point Terry had been wanting to make was that he was no longer able to look after the mausoleum – that, rather than the question of his doubts, was what he was trying to make clear to Tom.

'Of course that doesn't mean to say that we wouldn't be happy to assist if you were having another flower festival or anything like that,' Terry added. 'And we do weddings, as you know. Cheerio then, rector.'

Tom watched Terry drive off and returned to the church, where Miss Lee was doing what she called 'her' brasses and Miss Grundy attending to the flowers on the altar.

'I thought it was about time that young man put in an appearance,' said Miss Lee in a censorious tone. She was wearing old black cotton gloves, presumably to protect her hands from the metal polish, and her gestures with these gave her a sinister air.

'He probably won't be coming any more,' Tom found himself saying, though he had not intended to confide in Miss Lee.

'Oh, they're all the same now. Nobody wants to *work*,' she said fiercely.

The brasses had never looked more brilliant than now, in the November gloom, Tom thought, and he knew that it was hard rubbing that did it. But he felt disinclined to go into the subject of work with a retired gentlewoman as much out of touch as he was with the present industrial situation. So much of his life as rector

200

of a country parish seemed to be wasted in profitless discussions of this kind.

'I expect there'll be no difficulty in getting somebody else to do it,' he said lightly, but with a confidence he did not really feel. A competent agnostic with some knowledge of horticulture — was that all that was needed? Believer not objected to? Like a *Church Times* advertisement of the old days?

'Miss Vereker always took such a pride,' Miss Lee began, but Tom did not encourage her to go on. Instead, he found himself speculating on whether Miss Lee had ever had 'doubts'; if, when rubbing up the brass head of the eagle lectern, she had ever wondered whether the whole business wasn't an elaborate fiction and asked herself what she was doing here, Sunday after Sunday and even some weekdays, subscribing to something she wasn't sure about. Could he possibly ask her? he wondered, his eyes roving round the church and finding proof of her industry wherever he looked.

But it was while he was doing this that his glance fell on the lectern, the brazen bird of his imaginings, and he suddenly realised that it was not made of brass at all but of wood. It was an oak lectern made, according to an inaccurate local legend, from a tree on the de Tankerville estate. He must have been remembering some other lectern, probably the one in the church of his childhood. How could he have been so forgetful and unobservant! So now the question he put to Miss Lee was nothing to do with faith or lack of it but something much simpler. 'Do you ever wish we had a brass lectern?' he asked. 'As they have in some other churches?'

'Oh no, rector,' she answered. 'I *love* that old

wooden bird, and I *love* polishing it. A brass one may look more brilliant, but wood can be very rewarding, you know, and I think I can flatter myself that nobody can get a better polish on it than I do.'

Tom turned aside, humbled by her words. It was almost an idea for a sermon, what she had said about brass looking more brilliant but wood being very rewarding. Of course Miss Lee never had doubts! And if she ever had, she was much too well-bred ever to dream of troubling the rector with such a thing.

He made his way towards the altar where Miss Grundy was putting the finishing touches to an arrangement of roses.

'Roses in November, that's really something!' he said with forced heartiness, but he always felt obscurely guilty about Miss Grundy and so tended to behave unnaturally towards her. She was one of the people one ought to 'do' something about, though it was difficult to think what, added to which he was uncomfortably aware that the kind of services he conducted were not really to her liking.

'Oh, there are still roses out in our garden,' she said in her flutey voice, 'and I think these will do another week, with a few more leaves. A few green leaves can make such a difference.'

There was another crumb for a sermon, Tom thought, what with that and the rewarding qualities of wood. But it was somehow depressing the way these elderly women kept giving him ideas for sermons. He determined not to use them.

'You're so good with flowers and plants,' he said, picking on Miss Grundy's solitary talent. Perhaps she would be the one person who could raise corn from the grains of wheat found in the wrappings of a mummy. He had read in a local history book about something of the kind which had occurred in a village not twenty miles from here. If only one could get hold of a grain of this 'mummy wheat', Miss Grundy might come into her own!

26

All through her exile in West Kensington Miss Vereker
had cherished a memory of her early days as governess
to the girls at the manor, and before she died she
determined to pay a last visit to the village to see the
house again, the church, the mausoleum, and the few
people who still remembered her. She chose a beautiful
November day, with brilliant sunshine and the air
almost like spring, the kind of day that may suddenly
come in the unpredictable English autumn. She took
the train from Paddington to the station nearest to the
village, not telling her nephew and his wife what she
was doing. After all, she was just going for the day (half
price on her Senior Citizen's rail-card) and would be
back in the early evening. She wouldn't tell anyone in
the village either − just surprise them, perhaps for a
light lunch with Miss Lee, but she didn't want to think
of anyone taking trouble. A bit of bread and cheese
would do for her, what was jokingly called a
'ploughman's' lunch, herself being the most unlikely
ploughman you could possibly imagine (though hardly
more unlikely than those who habitually ordered it in
the pub where her nephew went).

She thought of her nephew as she sat in the train. Of

course in theory he would have been only too happy to take her wherever she wanted to go in the car, but in practice it never seemed to be the right time. To begin with, he could only manage a Saturday or a Sunday and there was always something else more urgent on Saturday, while Sunday morning was devoted to cleaning the car and the afternoon to visiting his wife's parents, like as not. Of course she was very lucky to have been 'taken in' like this; an aunt was not a very high priority on most people's lists of obligations, but she had been the favourite sister of her nephew's dead mother and in this way held in superstitious veneration. And then, of course, when she reached her seventies, though she was marvellous for her age apart from a touch of bronchitis in the winter, she became an old person and therefore entered yet another sacred category, that of 'the aged'. So, all in all, Miss Vereker had nothing to complain of in her present life, except that it was not the past.

After Oxford the train seemed to slow down as if there was no hurry now, no need to arrive anywhere at any particular time. It stopped at several places which Miss Vereker remembered from the old days, though the stations looked sadly neglected now, with no neat little gardens, only a tangle of weeds and grass with perhaps the remains of some more persistent plants which had seeded themselves. The 'family' would not have approved of this, she felt, as she got out and handed in the half of her ticket to a youth who seemed to be in charge of the station. There was, of course, no car from the big house to meet her, or indeed any car to take her anywhere, though there were a great many cars parked in the station yard, more than she ever remembered seeing. Presumably people used the station to go to work in Oxford or even in London, returning in the evening.

She set out to walk to the village. It was less than half a mile to the outskirts of the woods, and she could easily manage that. Then, after a pleasant stroll through the woods, with a sight of the house, she would arrive in the village to surprise Miss Lee or even Dr G. – not the rector, she was not acquainted with the present incumbent – there would surely be somebody who remembered her.

In the village, morning surgery was nearing its end – both Dr G. and Dr Shrubsole were having a busy morning. The waiting-room had been crowded with people who knew each other and might be surprised to meet in these circumstances, though it was not a reaction they could express. Conversation at these times was kept to a minimum – one did not talk in this place. Adam Prince and Emma, sitting at opposite ends of the room, he with his own copy of the *Daily Telegraph*, she with a battered copy of *Woman's Own*, dated some twelve months back, which she had picked up from the waiting-room table, acknowledged each other with a smile then immediately absorbed themselves in their reading. Adam read with growing indignation and dismay about women 'priests' ordained overseas, while Emma plodded through the sexual difficulties expressed by writers to the advice page. Could she perhaps have written in about her own unsatisfactory relationship with Graham to this sympathetic woman adviser? But there was so little to confide. Better, surely, to turn to the cookery pages where she might find ideas of what she might give Tom for supper, if she invited him again. The brightly coloured illustrations gave other kinds of food for thought.

Dr G. had started off his day in high spirits. A fine bright autumn morning, but there was quite a nip in the air and the days were certainly drawing in. The cosy comforting of these chilly nights might lead to a good crop of babies in the summer.... He was therefore disappointed when Adam Prince came into the surgery, looking the very picture of health, fat and sleek as a well-living neutered cat. What could be *his* trouble? he thought irritably as he greeted him in his usual genial way and asked him how he did.

Adam proceeded to tell him. 'I suppose you'd call it tension or stress – isn't that the fashionable word? And I've been suffering from insomnia – things seem to be "getting me down".' He smiled at the slang expression.

'Not sleeping, did you say?' Dr G. dismissed Adam's 'insomnia'. 'A warm milky drink at bedtime, perhaps ...,' he added vaguely, but even as he said it he realised that this remedy, the very idea of warmness and milkiness, would repel rather than help Adam Prince. Nor did one think of a man of his age as having a 'bedtime'.

'I *don't* think, in my case...,' Adam began.

'What sort of things worry you, get you down?' Dr G. asked.

'Oh, *well*...,' again Adam smiled. These 'things' were, of course, rather less serious than his doubting the validity of Anglican Orders or anything of that nature, but they *did* cause worry, tension, stress, whatever you liked to call it. Yet when you actually listed them they sounded trivial, mere pinpricks of

207

irritation. He proceeded to tell Dr G. about the unreasonable fury he felt at seeing a bottle of wine being warmed up ('chambréed') on a storage heater, or being offered vinegary bottled mayonnaise instead of home-made, or sliced bread or processed cheese, or there being no Dijon mustard available when asked for, or freshly ground coffee, and finally, the use of tea-bags – that seemed to upset him quite unreasonably.

Dr G. stopped him at this point – for the list threatened to be endless – to remind him that the use of tea-bags in restaurants was now universal, so very sensible and convenient and much less trouble for the womenfolk, avoiding *their* stress, you might say. 'It seems to me', he pronounced, 'that the sort of job you're doing is getting you down. You need a rest from it. All this going round eating meals and writing about them....' He seemed to reduce Adam's occupation to a very unimportant level. 'Well, it's not natural, is it?' He became bluff and hearty again. 'Try not to be quite so critical – learn to like processed cheese and tea-bags and instant coffee, and beefburgers and fish fingers too – most of the people in this village live on such things and they're none the worse for it. As for the sleeping or not sleeping – insomnia, I think you called it – well, as I've said, try not to be so critical – take a short brisk walk last thing at night, and a warm milky drink at bedtime takes a lot of beating. I often recommend it.' He did not feel it necessary to add that this was usually for young pregnant mums. When Adam murmured something about a prescription for sleeping tablets, Dr G. scribbled something, more in the nature of a placebo, repeated his advice to Adam not to worry, and dismissed him. He had seen Emma Howick in the waiting-room and a woman patient would surely be more interesting and rewarding than a pompous bore like Adam Prince.

But Emma was going to consult Martin Shrubsole and went into the other surgery, leaving Dr G. with a tiresome woman who only wanted her blood pressure taken.

Martin had so far had a difficult morning. He had been obliged to tell an elderly woman patient that her days were numbered, for, in his usual frank way, he had not shrunk from the truth. In his opinion it was no good trying to hide things from an intelligent person. But she had come back at him by asking if he believed in life after death. For a moment he had been stunned into silence, indignant at such a question. Then of course he had realised that *he* couldn't be expected to answer things like that – it was the rector's business. The fact that death came to all of us seemed irrelevant at this moment. It was a relief when she slipped quietly out of the room and Emma came in.

Emma had a slight rash on one of her hands, probably caused by some allergy – detergent, no doubt – though it might just possibly have some other cause – stress, perhaps – what did the doctor think?

At the mention of 'stress' Martin was at once on the alert. Although his main field of study and interest was geriatrics, he was well aware of the importance of giving full attention to *all* his patients, for even the young middle-aged would one day be old persons. Besides, he was interested in and puzzled by Emma, who did not seem to fit into any of his prearranged categories.

'Have you been in a particularly stressful situation lately?' he asked.

Emma seemed as if she might burst out laughing. 'Well, who hasn't, come to that,' she said. 'Life is full of stressful situations, isn't it?'

'Yes, the pace of life these days,' Martin began, but it did not seem strictly applicable to the village; obviously she must be referring to some particular aspect of her own life. That man in the cottage in the woods, Graham Pettifer (*Doctor* Pettifer), who had bored them all in the pub one evening, holding forth about something in Central Africa, could *he* be the cause of her stress? 'Even in a seemingly quiet life-style,' he went on, 'there can be stress.'

Emma agreed that there could be.

'Having to look after an aged relative, for instance. I've seen so much of it.'

'Yes, I expect you have,' said Emma sympathetically. 'You specialised in geriatric medicine, didn't you, before you came here?'

Martin said that he had, but it was getting to be the wrong way round, the patient questioning the doctor. Then he remembered that Emma was an anthropologist, or at least had been engaged in the kind of work that involved questioning people, so he felt less inadequate. He must press on and try to get to the root of her trouble. 'Let me see the hand,' he said.

Emma placed her right hand, palm downwards, on his.

'It seems rather rough,' he said. But was he insulting her, suggesting that she didn't take care of her hands, use hand-cream after washing as his wife and mother-in-law did? And there was such a difference in the feel of people's hands – a woman's, a child's, an old person's.... 'Sometimes an unsatisfactory relationship can cause stress,' he said boldly.

Emma looked up at his young earnest face, bending towards her. He was really making an effort to get to the cause of her trouble. 'I suppose I ought to wear rubber gloves when I'm washing up and that sort of thing,' she said.

'Yes, you could try that.' Perhaps it was a relief that she had rejected his invitation to confide. 'And I'll give you a prescription – come and see me again in three weeks if things don't improve.'

The way he had said 'things' left the situation open, wide open, really. She could confide her whole life to him, if need be.

Martin wondered if his wife would be able to get to the bottom of whatever it was and imagined them walking in the woods, Avice beating down nettles with her stick while Emma poured out her heart.

Emma left the surgery clutching her prescription – 'script', the junkies called it – grateful that he had not asked her about her sex life or lack of it.

That same morning, on the outskirts of Birmingham, Daphne was taking Bruce to the vet. The scene in the surgery waiting-room was very different from the hushed atmosphere at the doctors', with nobody speaking to anybody. Here there was a friendly air and anxious, even searching, enquiry into the ailments and troubles of the patients, cradled in their owners' arms or shrouded in baskets and boxes on the urine-stained carpet (the result of a nervous animal forgetting itself). Neutering and spaying, the best treatment for worms, the various injections against cat flu, distemper and hard pad were all fit subjects of conversation, eagerly discussed.

When Daphne's turn came she found that she was seeing the youngest of the vets — there were three in the practice — and that he had the same air of anxious concern that reminded her of Martin Shrubsole. His kindly manner as he prepared Bruce for his injection — 'Just a routine jab — this won't hurt you a bit, old chap' — made her feel that he would be sympathetic to her own troubles, even advise her what to do for the best. It was a gift some people had, a great asset, as much for a veterinary surgeon as for a general practitioner. How often must this young man have reassured and comforted worried and distressed owners, how many more years of such devoted caring lay before him! But of course she couldn't really confide in him in the same way she did in Martin Shrubsole, couldn't burden him with her own troubles — how Birmingham, even the house on the outskirts of the delightful wooded common, wasn't really proving to be the answer, was really no substitute for the stark white cottage on the shores of the Aegean. And then there was Heather — how much bossier she had become in her old age — and Tom — she sometimes worried about Tom and whether he was getting on all right, and had she done the right thing in leaving him as she had.... But none of this could be revealed to the sympathetic young vet.

'Come on, Bruce,' she said, 'let the doctor take your paw.'

The vet laughed. 'Funny, my name's Bruce too,' he said.

It seemed to create a bond between them and she felt almost as if she really *had* confided her worries to him. But all she said was what a shame it was the way you were always seeing notices everywhere about dogs not

212

being welcome in places. Bruce was so well behaved, would never do anything he ought not to. Not like a cat.

'Oh no,' he agreed. 'You can't tell a *cat* not to do anything. Did you ever have a cat?'

'No,' she said, 'though I think my brother would have liked one,' she added, a shadow crossing her face at the thought of Tom.

'They shall wax old as doth a garment,' Tom read. *Lanatus* – buried in wool. Wool, being an animal fibre, would decay, would it not? So there would be little or no trace of the statutory 'woollen' in which all were obliged to be buried according to the edict of August 1678. How long *did* wool take to decay? he wondered. He could not recall any instance of fragments of wool having been found when a grave of the period had been opened and the bones taken out. Of course one did not know personally of anyone having been buried in woollen, apart from Miss Lickerish's hedgehog and that was hardly relevant.

Hunger gnawed at his vitals and he paused in his speculations. He believed that Mrs Dyer had left him some cold meat for his lunch, and there was a tin of soup to be heated up. *She* would know, perhaps, how long wool took to decay, and also what people were buried in nowadays, what shrouds were made of. Hadn't she a distant relative who worked in a funeral parlour? Mrs Dyer would certainly know all about 'man-made' fibres. But he shrank from asking her.

Over his lunch he read the back page of the *Daily Telegraph*, the newspaper Daphne had preferred and which was still delivered at the rectory. So many people dying, he read, and none of them buried in woollen! The act had been repealed early in the nineteenth century, as far as he remembered, but there was nothing to stop a person being buried in woollen now if he so desired – a note in a will to that effect.... He ate cold lamb and bread and crunched pickled onions, his eyes moving mechanically and alphabetically down the list of deaths. *Driver, Fabian Charlesworth*, he read. *'Devoted husband of Constance and Jessie ...'* an odd way of putting it. Had the man had two wives still living? Tom wondered. And had they got together after the man's death? And where would he be buried – with the first wife or the second?

There was still room in the churchyard here for his own burial, he reflected, if he should go suddenly. He was forgetting for the moment that Laura had been buried elsewhere. But supposing *he* were to marry again, as this man Driver must have done, what would be the position then?

27

It was colder walking in the woods than it had been
sitting in the train, but it was still a bright day and the
slightly uphill walk from the station was invigorating.
Miss Vereker wasn't exactly cold, it was just that the
unaccustomed exertion – her West Kensington walks
being mainly on the flat – had made her conscious of a
sharp pain in her back and she was finding it difficult to
breathe. The air this morning had seemed almost mild,
but now there was a cutting wind coming at her
through the trees.

She stopped for a minute to have a rest. This, surely,
was the cottage where Clegg, one of the keepers, used
to live; but it looked in a sad state now, the garden
neglected and the curtains in the front windows
obviously in need of a wash. Miss Vereker peered, in a
way she would normally have thought discourteous,
but it didn't matter since the cottage was clearly
uninhabited. Where did the keepers live now then?
Probably in some modern bungalow or council house,
the wives not caring for the isolation of the woods. A
cup of tea or a glass of Mrs Clegg's elderberry wine,
which would have been offered in the old days, would
be welcome now, but there was no hope of that. She

must go on, 'press on regardless', as her nephew was fond of saying. It couldn't be so very far to the village and she would soon get through the woods. Looking at her watch, she saw that it was half-past one – not a very suitable time to call on anybody. She was surprised to see that it was so late – she must have stopped longer by the cottage than she had realised.

She walked on with her usual determination, back upright and head held high. The path was clear enough though it was rather overgrown, more than it used to be. Still, this *was* the path, there was no doubt about that. It was only that the pain in her back was sharper and more continuous now, reminding her of that time when she had had a touch of pleurisy and the doctor had listened with his stethoscope, hearing what he described as a noise like dry leaves rubbing together, the kind of noise she was hearing now as she took a breath, or was it only the rustle of the fallen leaves on the path?

She realised that she was beginning to walk more slowly. Perhaps it was farther than she had remembered, and now she seemed to have strayed some way off the direct path on to a muddier track, much trodden down by hoof marks, either of cows or horses. The girls had sometimes come riding here and no doubt people still did. She wished she had thought of bringing a stick with her; it would have been useful, not so much to support her faltering steps, she told herself jokingly, as to push aside some of the branches and brambles that were getting in her way. It was so long since she had walked in this wood, or indeed in any wood, that she had forgotten how useful a stick could be.

And now she found herself in a kind of open clearing where there was a scattering of large stones, the kind one could sit down on for a brief rest. Not that she was really tired, it was only this annoying pain and − more important − the inadvisability of calling on Miss Lee and Miss Grundy at two o'clock in the afternoon. Miss Lee was the kind of person who had a 'rest' and might not welcome an unexpected visitor, even an old friend from the past.

'Mummy always has a little sleep after lunch,' Avice Shrubsole was saying, 'though she swears she doesn't. She begins by listening to *The Archers*, but before *Woman's Hour*'s started she's dropped off.' Avice laughed. '*I* like to get out for a walk when I can so I creep out and leave her, though Martin's always telling Mummy it would do her the world of good to get out into the woods.'

'I'm sure he is,' Emma murmured. Avice was the last person she had expected or wished to meet at such a time and in such circumstances and she had been unable to pretend that she was going in the opposite direction, had not thought quickly enough − for, after all, she had just been standing, mooning about, one could say − and Avice had looked at her sharply and suggested that it was a bit cold for hanging about (though a lovely bright day for November). So there they were walking briskly away from the village, Avice beating down the undergrowth on either side of the path with her stick.

'I gather you and Martin had an encounter this morning,' Avice said in a pleasant, friendly way, for of course one did not reveal that one knew about the visit

217

to the surgery, and he had apparently seen Emma getting petrol at the garage.

'Yes – and I went to the surgery about this rash on my hands,' Emma admitted.

'Oh really? That's a bore for you – I suppose it's detergents.'

'Yes, it might be. Or some darker secret might be causing it, stress and that sort of thing – you know what is said.'

'Of course!'

They both laughed and Avice struck a particularly fierce blow with her stick at a clump of harmless vegetation. Without revealing any secrets, for he was scrupulous about that kind of thing, Martin had said something about Emma being the kind of person who might 'need help' and hinted that Avice might be able to supply it. This looked like being just such an opportunity.

'Did you wonder why I was wandering aimlessly in the woods?' Emma asked.

Avice was taken aback at her approach. 'I assumed you were taking exercise,' she said.

'But you must have guessed about Graham and me, what there was or wasn't – you may even have heard what was said in the village.'

'I don't think anything was *said*, exactly....'

'Oh well, if there wasn't anything, that makes the whole thing even more humiliating.'

Emma seemed prepared to leave it at that, making it difficult for Avice to know how best to give the 'help' Martin had suggested Emma might need. But perhaps humiliation was something to latch on to – could Emma not be persuaded to enlarge on this?

'Maybe you expected too much,' she ventured.

'Oh, I didn't *expect* anything − what right had I to expect anything?' said Emma fiercely.

This seemed an unprofitable line to pursue and Avice decided that she would tell Martin that Emma's trouble was nothing more interesting than frustrated sex or even unrequited love for that man they had all thought rather a bore, though there was no accounting for tastes. Yet, as a woman, Avice felt that this might be over-simplifying the matter. She did not know how to proceed except by remarking that we never got all that we hoped for out of life and throwing in a hint of her own troubles. Shared confidences might lead to something.

'Yes, of course,' Emma agreed. 'Even the happily married woman with a nice considerate husband and splendid children might still feel that something was lacking. If she'd given up a promising career for these domestic things − as a concert pianist or a TV personality or even a social worker....'

It seemed to Avice that Emma was being deliberately mocking.

'Well, it *is* possible to do one's own thing, even with a husband and children,' Avice said defiantly, and of course she did do a lot of useful voluntary work in the district. 'But there are other problems,' she went on. 'Where one lives, for example. Our present house is much too small, especially now that Mummy's living with us.'

'Yes, I suppose it is. Let me see now' − Emma was making an effort − 'you can't have more than four bedrooms in your present house.'

'No. There's our room, of course − the boys share at

present, and Hannah has the little room in the front and Mummy is in what was the spare room.'

'And that's the four rooms accounted for,' Emma agreed. 'So you haven't a spare room, and if anyone comes to stay....'

'Exactly! There's just nowhere to put them.'

'And it's so awful sleeping in somebody's sitting-room surrounded by stuffed armchairs and standard lamps.'

'We do have a kind of put-u-up in the dining-room....'

'Oh, sleeping in somebody's dining-room would be even worse! Of course, you could turn your mother out – oh, I don't mean literally,' Emma suggested. 'Would she perhaps like a small cottage in the village, if one was available, or one of those new bungalows opposite the church? That might be a solution.'

Avice smiled, remembering the conversation they had had when Tom had come to supper. 'You know what the real solution would be?' she said.

'For you to get a bigger house, obviously – though you wouldn't want to leave here, would you?'

'There would be no need to leave here – not if we lived at the rectory.' Avice's stick slashed so furiously at an overhanging branch that she might have been cutting down Tom himself.

'But how could you do that? What about the rector – where would he go? Hardly to one of the bungalows opposite the church!'

'No, of course not.' Avice proceeded to explain about over-large rectories and vicarages and how so many clergy now lived in smaller and more convenient houses. Now that Daphne had gone, a cottage could be found for Tom, or even a small house on the housing estate. It was a mistake to associate the clergy only with large ancient vicarages and rectories, quite against the modern trend which was all for the clergy being in closer touch with their parishioners, more like ordinary people, altogether less isolated and set apart. Why, she had even heard of one London vicar who lived in a tower block! Avice was sure Tom would be much happier out of the rectory.

'Happier? One doesn't somehow think of him as being *happy*,' Emma began, but what might have been an interesting and profound conversation was broken into by Avice pointing with her stick and exclaiming, 'Why, look! There's an old woman lying there in that clearing – do you see?'

'Good heavens, so there is! Is she asleep or ill? And who is she? Certainly not a tramp, to judge by her appearance.'

She was a tall woman, as far as one could judge, dressed in a long coat of some ancient fur, the kind of coat she had obviously had many years before people were sensitive about wearing the skins of animals and a musquash coat could be bought for £20. The coat was pushed back to reveal a jersey suit of a patterned blue and brown design, a good Liberty silk scarf, ribbed woollen stockings and short brown ankle boots. By her side was a handbag and a pair of gloves, both apparently 'good' brown leather rather than plastic. She had evidently been wearing a blue felt hat which had slipped off her head and was now lying by a stone. The face, when they were able to inspect it more closely, was of a grey-haired woman in her seventies, wearing glasses and apparently asleep. At the approach

221

of Avice and Emma she seemed to wake up and make some attempt to tidy herself, even to rise to her feet, reaching for her hat and gloves and beginning to explain who she was, what she was doing and why she was in the woods. But she seemed confused and in some distress, obviously in need of help.

An old person for Martin Shrubsole and something for Avice to do also, Emma thought, and went to get her car.

28

The telephone rang in the rectory study with the startling suddenness of breaking in on a profound or irrelevant thought. Tom had been considering the gospel for the last Sunday after Trinity — 'Stir-up Sunday', as it was called — and wondering how Adam Prince, in his Anglican days, had dealt with the miracle of the five barley loaves and two small fishes. What sort of a sermon had he preached on that text and what sort would he preach now, with his wider culinary experience?

Tom picked up the telephone and heard the excited tones of an elderly man. He did not at first realise that it was Dr G. speaking, for he and the doctor did not often communicate by telephone.

'I thought you ought to know', the voice said, 'that Miss Vereker has been found wandering in the woods.'

Wandering in the woods ... how beautiful that sounded, with its Anglo-Saxon alliteration. But who was 'Miss Vereker' and why should her wanderings concern him, be something that he 'ought' to know about?

'Miss Lilian Vereker,' Dr G. repeated, 'found wandering in the woods.'

'Yes, so you said.' Tom was racking his brains. 'Should one be...?'

'I thought you ought to be informed, as rector — though of course it was before your time. Miss Vereker was the governess at the manor, you remember....'

'Ah *yes*!' Miss Vereker taught the girls, those legendary figures, the bright young things, as they afterwards became....

'Martin Shrubsole is coping — he and Avice will know the best thing to do.'

'Anything *I* can do?' Tom felt bound to ask. He wondered if Miss Vereker had expressed a wish to see the rector, demanded the services of a priest.

'Well, it seems rather more in our line than yours,' Dr G. said. 'Martin feels that Miss Vereker may be in need of psychiatric help — you know that's the first thing these young men think of now — but she seems perfectly *compos mentis* to me. Just a touch of bronchitis, in my opinion. Apparently she got off the train and began to walk from the station through the woods. No harm in that — if only more people would walk! Apparently Miss Howick was there too and went for her car — she and Avice had been walking together — a lucky thing — when they came upon Miss Vereker....'

All these people walking in the woods! Dr G. was right — we should all do more of it. He brushed aside a confused memory of his evening walk with Emma and his own wanderings in search of the remains of the D.M.V. 'I'd better come along,' he said.

When he arrived at the Shrubsoles' house Tom found that tea had been made and that the doctor's mother-in-law was cutting a large iced cake.

'Miss Vereker was found wandering in the woods,' Avice said, as if Tom might not have heard.

'You were taking a walk?' Tom asked politely.

'Exactly! "Wandering" gives quite the wrong idea, doesn't it. I was taking what I remembered as a short cut to the village from the station and strayed off the path.' Miss Vereker, sitting upright in a chair by the fire, gave a short laugh. 'So perhaps in that sense I *was* wandering.'

Tom found himself thinking of 'Lead Kindly Light', but Newman, he recalled, had been on a boat becalmed in the straits of Bonifacio when he wrote the poem that became the hymn, not lost in an English wood.

'I saw this pile of stones, quite large ones,' Miss Vereker went on, 'so I decided to sit down and rest on one of them.'

'The woods are full of stones,' said Avice, forestalling any possible questioning from Tom about the exact location and nature of these particular stones. It would be just like him to be more interested in his wretched deserted medieval village than the problems of an elderly person in trouble. 'I think Miss Vereker should rest now,' she said firmly, 'after all this excitement,' so of course Tom could not in all decency pursue the question of the stones.

That same evening there was a power cut which lasted from 6.30 to 9, disrupting the lives and television viewing of most people in the village. Luckily most of them had already done their cooking for their unfashionably early evening meals.

Emma had not started to cook when the power failed, and her supper consisted of gin and tonic and

225

boiled eggs and toast done on the fire. What could be better? she asked herself, settling down contentedly. She almost rang Tom to find out if he was managing but, remembering her recent experience with Graham, decided against any precipitate action.

Tom had also had recourse to drink — the remains of a last Christmas bottle of whisky from Dr G. came in handy and he found some bread and cheese, proud of himself for such resourcefulness. Also, investigating the cupboard in the sideboard with a torch, he came upon a bottle of apricot brandy, unbroached — where had *that* come from? — and it occurred to him that it might be a suitable present or bribe for the organist, perhaps even induce him to play at Evensong in the winter months. He would lay it quietly at his door one day — no need to mention it at the parochial church council meeting. By candlelight he took out the diary he had been attempting to keep since Daphne went, noting the events of the day — and it had been quite a day! — and adding one or two observations of his own. He was not consciously setting out to emulate Woodforde or Kilvert, but it would be a pity if the clergy of today were too taken up with social work to record the daily trivia that might be of interest to the historian of the twenty-first century. He was still writing and had just reached his speculations about the possible location of the D.M.V., linked with the finding of Miss Vereker, when the lights came on again.

Miss Lee and Miss Grundy were only temporarily disconcerted when the lights failed and the television screen went dark. The excitement of the day had been almost too much for Miss Lee, with the promise of seeing Miss Vereker again in the morning, and she and

Miss Grundy had an early light meal before watching *Crossroads*. But they soon settled themselves resignedly by the fire, fingers busy with knitting and crochet. The old coped better than the young in these circumstances. It was not outside the bounds of possibility to boil a kettle on the fire or even to cook on a paraffin stove. There were always candles in the house and you could listen to the wireless if your thoughts didn't supply enough entertainment.

Adam Prince was perhaps the only person who might have been seriously inconvenienced, for he was preparing a rather special dinner for the priest of the Roman Catholic church he attended. But he had already made the salmon mousse, and the *boeuf en daube* and the jacket potatoes (good English–French tradition food) had been cooking slowly for two hours when the power went off, and would continue to simmer in the oven for some time. As for the cheeses – specially bought in the market in Oxford that morning – they would come to no harm, and there was always plenty to drink. Indeed, just as the coffee stage was reached the power came on again.

'The light has been restored, thank God!' said Father Byrne in his rich Abbey Theatre tones, giving the announcement an almost religious significance. 'And no harm done.'

In the next-door cottage Miss Lickerish had not bothered to put on the light at the normal time. She boiled a kettle on the fire and then sat in her chair with a cup of tea at her side and a cat on her knees. But some time during those dark hours the cat left her and sought the warmth of his basket, Miss Lickerish's lap having become strangely chilled.

*

Miss Vereker lay in a hard, child's bed in a strange room in Dr Shrubsole's house. It had been kind of them to put her up, but she would have preferred to stay with Miss Lee. One of the children here had been obliged to turn out of her room and sleep in the sitting-room, the house being really too small to accommodate an extra person. In the old days, of course, this had been only a cottage where one of the gardeners had lived and now, even with that rather ugly 'extension' stuck on at the side, it still wasn't big enough for the Shrubsole family. There was something curiously wrong about the way houses were arranged now – small ones crammed with people and large ones, like the manor, almost empty or occupied only at weekends, or, even worse, turned into flats. And now this power cut – adding insult to injury, you might say, though of course Mrs Shrubsole was most efficient and had provided an excellent supper. It had been suggested that she should visit the manor, but she was not sure that she wanted that, with all the changes now and her memories. But she was sure of one thing – tomorrow she would pay a visit to the mausoleum. That was always the same.

29

With Miss Lickerish's death, Tom felt that he came into his own. If he had been conscious of inadequacy in the matter of Miss Vereker, it was now obvious that there were some situations that only the clergy could manage properly. The doctors had done their part and it was now over to Tom. He reflected that had Miss Vereker been found dead, instead of merely resting on a stone, the doctors would have left him to it, with Miss Vereker beyond the need even of psychiatric help.

'Miss Lickerish's gone!' There was the familiar triumphant note in Mrs Dyer's tone as she announced the death in the post office. Emma, who had been buying stamps, recognised it as the same note that had been in her voice when she had informed Emma and her mother that they wouldn't find many blackberries where they had chosen to pick. Emma had already noticed Mrs Dyer's son Jason hovering near Miss Lickerish's cottage, like some vulture, with his lank shoulder-length hair and spindly jean-clad legs. Presumably he was waiting hopefully to pounce on whatever 'effects' the old woman had left, practically everything being saleable and 'collectable' now.

'Had Miss Lickerish any relatives here?' Emma

asked in her innocent way, which produced another triumphant snort from Mrs Dyer. Apparently the village was full of them — Miss Lickerish had several nephews and nieces living on the new estate. 'Catch *them* coming to see their old auntie!'

Emma hoped that it would be in order for her to attend the funeral — essential for her village 'research', after all. And when she had found out that she might even be expected to attend — as a mark of she was not quite sure what — the question of flowers worried her. Would it be the done thing to send some, a bunch or spray of whatever happened to be in season? Miss Lickerish's relatives were unlikely to specify 'garden flowers only' — which would hardly have been practicable in November — or request donations to a charity, though something to do with animals would have been appropriate for Miss Lickerish. Country people in general probably didn't regard animals on a level with human beings — was that perhaps an upper-class concept?

On the morning of the funeral Emma saw that people were going down to Miss Lickerish's cottage with flowers, so she took her own bunch of florist's-shop carnations and followed what seemed to be the approved pattern.

When she got there she found that two smartly dressed young women, whom she took to be the nieces, were sitting in the front room, a rather formal type of parlour, barred to the cats and hedgehogs, preparing to receive the flowers. The nieces wore bright colours — nobody went in for mourning these days, Emma knew — and one of them was surreptitiously smoking a cigarette, holding it down concealed in her fingers.

Emma's flowers were graciously received and she was invited to inspect the other tributes. The nieces seemed especially pleased with a wreath of white and yellow chrysanthemums, brought by the agent on behalf of the manor, and there was another wreath, of mauve everlastings and white carnations, from Dr and Mrs G. Adam Prince had sent a large sheaf of pink and white carnations wrapped in polythene.

In the church Emma was able to pick out a group of what were presumably relatives in the front pews, rather crowded together considering the amount of space there was in the rest of the building. Miss Vereker, who had known Miss Lickerish when she had worked at the manor, had stayed on for a few days with Miss Lee and Miss Grundy in order to attend the funeral. She appeared to have completely recovered from her ordeal and was looking around her with a proprietory air. Emma had placed herself towards the back of the church but with a good view of everything that was going on. When Tom entered with the coffin she experienced a feeling almost of emotion, but perhaps it was only the beautiful words of the burial service that moved her and how well Tom looked and spoke them.

The singing was hearty. The relatives' ideas for suitable hymns had been conventional, but Tom had dissuaded them from choosing 'Thy Way, not mine, O Lord', as its wormlike submission was totally unsuited to Miss Lickerish's personality ('Choose Thou for me my friends' – the very idea of it!). He had allowed 'Brief life is here our portion' – nobody could dispute that – and had included 'The God of Love my Shepherd is', in George Herbert's version.

Emma followed the mourners into the churchyard where the grave had been prepared and stood with the little group watching the earth falling on to the coffin. She was glad that it would not slide away into the flames, as at a cremation. All those flowers — the wreaths, the bunches, the sheafs — would be left to moulder away, to grow sodden with rain and decay as those of earlier burials had done, until they were finally thrown away into the wire basket where the dead church flowers were disposed of. Flowers from a funeral were perhaps not sent to patients in hospital or residents in old people's homes, as flowers from a wedding sometimes were? This might be an interesting variation of custom, Emma felt, something for noting in her paper 'Funeral Customs in a Rural Community'.

Afterwards, as everybody knew, the natural grief and tension of the occasion would be relaxed in the universal comfort of cups of tea, leading on to the more powerful solace of alcohol. Those who did not expect to join with the mourners in this extension of the funeral rites had grouped themselves near the mausoleum and Emma saw that Miss Vereker went inside it. She herself walked slowly home, noticing the progress made on the new bungalows opposite the church (a home for Tom?) and the old shrouded motor-cars in the orchard, now more clearly visible through the leafless trees.

Yet another extension of the funeral obsequies was to be observed in church on the Sunday after the funeral, when one of the front pews was occupied by a group of Miss Lickerish's relatives. They sat stiffly in a row, rather more squashed together than was usual among more regular churchgoers, leaning forward in the prayers rather than kneeling, hands shading their eyes. Apparently, as Emma learned afterwards from Tom, it was customary for the mourners to be present in church on the Sunday after the funeral. These particular people would not be seen at a service again until the next funeral, marriage or christening. When Emma expressed indignation, Tom, in his kinder and more tolerant way, pointed out that it gave a kind of continuity to village life, like the seasons – the cutting and harvesting of the crops, then the new sowing and the springing up again.

'I wish I'd known – but the funeral will be over now,' Daphne said. 'I could have gone if Tom had let me know in time.'

'She wasn't a friend of yours, surely, that odd old woman?' Heather was at her most brisk. She often found it necessary to adopt this tone with Daphne to stop her brooding and repining.

'Not a *friend* – Miss Lickerish didn't have friends in the way we think of friends. Only her cats and the hedgehogs, and once even a toad....' And, in a way, you could see her point – animals did not disappoint or deceive, perhaps because one expected less of them. One would not be led to expect *anything* from a hedgehog or a cat....

'I've never been a cat person,' said Heather complacently, 'and of course hedgehogs are full of fleas.'

'Tom's letter was full of news,' Daphne went on. 'What do you think, the old governess, the person who used to be governess at the manor, was found wandering in the woods. And Tom *thinks* that she may have stumbled on the remains of the D.M.V.'

'Goodness, that *would* be something, wouldn't it?' said Heather. 'He *must* be pleased.' Tiresome man, she thought, and a disappointment as an eligible widower. 'Those people opposite, the mother and daughter,' she added in a brighter tone, 'are having a Tupperware party next Wednesday evening and have asked us to go along.' She smiled. 'I know it isn't really our kind of entertainment — if you can call it entertainment — but we may as well be friendly, and they've got those two dogs and they'd know about the dog-training classes. They drive that yellow car, with the dog grille over the back window.'

'Yes, of course, I've seen them.' Daphne wondered what the evening entertainment in a Greek village would have been. Presumably not a Tupperware party, though the Greeks were by no means unaware of the advance of modern technology. All those plastic bags on the seashore and she had once seen a priest carrying a blue plastic bag, but all that seemed very far away now, as if it had never been.

30

Christmas brought Beatrix and Isobel to the cottage, and Emma resigned herself to a quiet female celebration of the festival with decorous eating and drinking. There seemed little prospect of any other form of entertainment.

'We could have asked that friend of yours, Ianthe Potts,' Beatrix said, when it was too late to do anything about it. 'Would you have liked that?'

'No,' said Emma, remembering Ianthe's summer visit.

Beatrix did not improve matters by asking Emma whether she thought Graham and Claudia would be spending Christmas together in their new house in Islington. Christmas *was* the time when people tended to come together, was it not, she declared, in her usual dry way.

The post that morning had brought a card from Graham. 'With love' had been added in his handwriting to the printed message. Emma stood fingering the card, wondering if there was any significance in the fact that he had chosen to send her a woodland scene (in aid of the Foresters' or Gardeners' Benevolent Fund). Could it be regarded as a subtle reminder of the time he had spent in the cottage in the

woods? But men were not usually subtle in *that* way –
women were too apt to read into their actions things
that were never even thought of, let alone intended.

'That's an attractive card,' Beatrix said. 'Not entirely
suitable for Christmas, perhaps, but an agreeable
picture. Did Claudia choose it?'

Emma now saw that it probably was so. Wives did
buy cards for their husbands, even sent them out.

'He might have sent you a present, considering all
you did for him,' Beatrix said.

Emma had thought of this too but preferred not to
put it into words. 'I didn't do all that much,' she said.

'You helped him find the cottage, which helped him
to finish his book – you consoled him when he was
estranged from his wife – I'm sure you did some
cooking. I think that's a good deal.'

'And yet it's all relative – look how much more Miss
Vereker did for Tom by stumbling on the site of the
D.M.V., quite unconsciously,' Emma said.

'Of course he knows such a lot about these things,'
said Isobel dutifully. 'Was his wife interested in history
when she was alive? It must have been a bond between
them.'

'I suppose it could have been, though one hopes
there was more than that between them. Perhaps he
only took to history after her death, but we hardly
know anything about poor Laura, do we?' Beatrix
turned to Emma.

'I don't know anything more than you do,' said
Emma, almost indignant. 'She died such a long time
ago – I think he hardly remembers her now.'

'That seems rather a lot to know,' said Beatrix, 'as if
you had talked about it.'

'Oh, I think we did just mention it one evening,' said Emma casually.

'Just mention...,' Beatrix repeated.

'I should have thought it was a mistake his sister leaving him like that,' said Isobel. 'A clergyman does need a woman about the place to see to things, in the parish as well as in the house. It isn't as if he would ever marry again, is it?'

'Who are we to know that?' said Beatrix. 'When Laura died, Daphne was on the spot so quickly that he didn't have a chance to think what he wanted to do, but now it might be different.'

Isobel looked almost embarrassed, as if she might be somehow involved, but said nothing.

'After all, widowers usually do marry again,' Beatrix went on.

'I haven't really known many widowers,' Emma said, appearing to dismiss the subject. Graham did not come into that category and Tom, being the rector of the parish, hardly seemed in her eyes to count as an eligible man. Yet in some respects there was no doubt that he might be regarded as such.

'You must have nearly finished your writing-up now,' said Isobel firmly, as if interviewing Emma about her future, 'so I dare say you'll be going back to London to start another project?'

Emma said nothing. It seemed too much to have to think beyond Christmas and to consider anything as unattractive-sounding as 'another project'. But she must never forget that Isobel was a headmistress of the old-fashioned type – there was still the hint of the stern but kindly gleam behind the pince-nez.

'If you don't want to stay here after Christmas,'

Beatrix said, 'there *is* one of my old students who might be glad to rent the cottage. She's recovering from an unsatisfactory love affair and writing a novel.'

Emma laughed. '*Just* the kind of person to come and live here,' she said. 'And if Daphne comes back from Birmingham, they could get together and compare notes on blighted hopes.'

'Oh, I don't think we want *that* to happen − not Daphne coming back,' said Beatrix firmly. 'Tom's life must go in some other direction now.'

Looking round the church for the midnight service (he did not dare to call it 'Mass') Tom was pleased to see that there was a larger congregation than usual. He was especially glad about this because one of his Christmas cards had taken the form of a 'newsletter' from an old friend which, with its catalogue of achievements of himself, his wife and their five children, had made Tom feel more than usually inadequate. And now the entry of Sir Miles and his party from the manor coincided with a magnificent burst of sound from the organist playing Messiaen. In spite of being a church organist, Geoffrey Poore was not a believer, but he appreciated the opportunity of playing on a fine instrument, like some Jane Austen heroine, Jane Fairfax, perhaps, and her gift of a pianoforte. Tom, feeling the Messiaen engulf him, wondered if it could be the effect of the apricot brandy which he had laid on the organist's doorstep as a Christmas present. Certainly the building was filled with unusually splendid sound which gave a grandeur to the occasion.

Emma, taking note of the party from the manor, wondered if they had earlier welcomed carol singers with mulled wine and mince pies. No doubt Miss Lee would know what had been done in the old days. Emma, sitting between her mother and Isobel, found herself wishing that she had a man with her, though the idea of the man being Graham did not appeal to her. Some nebulous, comfortable – even handsome – figure suggested itself, which made her realise that even the most cynical and sophisticated woman is not, at times, altogether out of sympathy with the ideas of the romantic novelist.

'Of course you'll be wanting to go to church,' Heather said in an accusing tone.

'Well yes, I think so,' Daphne agreed, but with a marked lack of enthusiasm. Naturally she would want to go to church at Christmas but she was not particularly attracted to either of the nearby churches, both of which she had attended on various occasions. One was unashamedly high, with stifling clouds of incense and the service conducted in a rapid mumble that she found difficult to follow, while the other was excessively evangelical, too light and too bright, with a welcome from the smiling vicar that was more than she could stand. This vicar also had a dog and was sometimes seen on the common, tweedily dressed but instantly recognisable as a clergyman. So going to church was not as easy as might appear. In the end she chose the dark crowded Midnight Mass of the higher church, while Heather waited up rather grimly in her housecoat and hairnet, complaining that she couldn't possibly sleep until Daphne came in. She would lie awake listening for her key in the lock, and of course Bruce would bark.

On Boxing Day Daphne wondered, not for the first time, whether it had been a mistake leaving Tom, 'to his own devices', as she put it, especially at a time like Christmas. Was it not her duty as an elder sister to keep an eye on him, even if not to help him in the parish? She began to plan a visit, after the New Year when the weather improved. Bruce could safely be left with Heather for a few days.

31

Daphne's New Year visit coincided with a Friday evening meeting of the history society which Tom had arranged to take place at the rectory. His first thought on her arrival was not so much pleasure at seeing his sister again as relief that she would be able to make the coffee which was usually provided on these occasions.

Daphne's first thought on entering the rectory was how cold it seemed after the kindly warmth of centrally heated Birmingham. And why hadn't Tom switched on the radiator in the hall?

'You'll have to get it warmer than this for the meeting tomorrow,' she said. 'Who's the speaker?'

'Dr G.,' said Tom.

'Whatever can *he* have to say?'

'He's promised to give an informal talk about the history of medicine, starting in the seventeenth century and working up to date – and he's got quite a good collection of old surgical instruments.'

'I don't think people will like *that*,' said Daphne doubtfully. 'What gave you the idea?'

'I was visiting the hospital and that set me thinking about death and how people died in the old days.' Once, during such a time, even when he was at the bed of a patient, he had found his thoughts going back to Anthony à Wood and his total suppression of urine – 'if thou canst not make water thou hadst better make earth'.... He had spoken before now with Dr G. about this and speculated on the nature of Wood's complaint. Dr G. had seemed pleased to be invited to give a talk to the society – it seemed to emphasise his rightful place in the village in a way that Tom had not acknowledged before.

Adam Prince was one of the first to arrive for the meeting and chose a good seat near the fire which Daphne had lit in the drawing-room. Next came Beatrix with Isobel and Emma, then Miss Lee and Miss Grundy and the usual group of elderly women from a nearby village, Tom's devoted helpers and copiers of parish registers. Magdalen Raven came rather late – there had been some last-minute crisis with the children – but Dr G.'s wife Christabel came even later, arriving with her husband and sitting in the front of the room. As the only woman wearing a long skirt (of wine-coloured velvet), she felt justified in looking around her critically, not so much at what the other women were wearing as at her surroundings in the rectory drawing-room. There was some good furniture (though in need of polishing), but the bowl of hyacinths, now a little past their best, seemed to her an inadequate flower decoration for the time of year. Beech leaves could have been preserved in glycerine and there was so much in the autumn gardens and hedgerows that could have been gathered and dried for winter use. But Daphne had been away – though she must have started the hyacinth bulbs before she went – there had been no woman at the rectory these last months, apart from the doubtful ministrations of Mrs Dyer. It showed, the absence of a woman of taste, though poor Daphne had never been *that*....

Beatrix had temporarily forgotten that Daphne was returning for a visit to her brother, and the sight of her in one of her baggy jumble-sale tweed skirts, standing awkwardly in the doorway, welcoming people as if she were still hostess at the rectory, filled her with dismay. This was *not* how things should be....

Now Tom stood up and introduced Dr G. (who of course needed no introduction), and Dr G. began his talk.

Looking around at his audience, he saw that it was predominantly elderly, the kind of audience that should have been addressed by Martin Shrubsole, who he noticed was not present tonight. But he was glad not to have to answer possible questions from the younger doctor, not to have to 'cross swords with him', as he put it, on certain areas of disagreement. For the talk, contrary to Tom's hopes, was not so much a history of medical practice from the seventeenth century as a harking back to the 'good old days' of the nineteen thirties before the introduction of the National Health Service — before the days when everybody had a motor-car and would even walk to the surgery from the next village. If only people would *walk* more — Dr G. emphasised his favourite topic — get out into the country, go into the woods, the surgery would be practically empty! He was glad to notice that some younger men were taking up the practice of 'jogging', as he believed it was called — it was a fine sight to see them trotting along on a winter morning. Ladies could do it too, no harm in that, but under medical supervision, of course. We couldn't have ladies dropping down dead, could we...?

There was a ripple of laughter from his audience, Emma observed, and it occurred to her that Dr G. might joke about elderly people dropping down dead because, being an old man and nearer his own end, he was obliged to make light of such things.

'So, ladies, only rather cautious jogging for you,' Dr G. repeated, and on that joking note he concluded his talk and invited questions.

Adam Prince got up to ask the first. He liked the idea of himself jogging – weather permitting, of course – but he knew better than to expose himself to ridicule by putting a question on the subject. Instead, he asked about diet in the old days and Dr G. was launched on another of his favourite topics, though it was difficult to gather from what he said whether diet was better then, with no frozen or 'convenience' foods, or worse because of lack of variety.

Tom tried to lead Dr G. back into earlier times, even Victorian medicine would be more appropriate to an historical talk, but Dr G. was not to be drawn. He had noticed Daphne and Miss Lee doing something with cups at the back of the room and suspected that it was time for coffee. People could examine his collection of surgical instruments if they wished. They were spread out on the table in the window and he would be happy to demonstrate their use if required. There was more laughter, and cups of coffee and plates of biscuits began to be handed round.

'*Not* quite all I'd hoped for,' said Tom to Beatrix, 'but I think people enjoyed it and I suppose that's the main thing. Isn't that what life's all about?' he added, hardly expecting an answer.

Beatrix felt herself unequal to making any comment

on this observation and left it to Isobel to remark that Tom must be glad to have his sister here.

'Glad?' Tom seemed to consider the meaning of the word before he answered quickly that yes, of course he was glad to have Daphne here. But he hardly knew what his feelings were at seeing his sister in her old place. They had not as yet spoken much about the purpose of her visit or gone more deeply into her life in Birmingham, though she had described the two churches to him and even asked his advice about which one he thought she should attend. That sounded as if she intended her stay in the house by the delightful wooded common to be a permanent one, as he had always understood. Yet at the back of his mind was the uneasy suspicion that people in the village expected Daphne to return one day. Also, he couldn't help remembering that she had not taken her bed with her.

'And how do you find the village?' Beatrix asked Daphne. 'In February it must seem bleak after Birmingham.'

'Oh, there can be bleakness in Birmingham,' said Daphne. 'I suppose February is a dreary month anywhere — except perhaps in warmer climes.' She used the deliberately stilted poetic phrase half jokingly, but it concealed her determination *not* to go to the cottage near Tintagel this summer but to have a holiday in Greece again.

'I expect the rectory strikes cold,' said Beatrix, also using an emotive phrase. 'You have central heating in your new house, I imagine?'

'Oh, yes, but...,' Daphne hesitated, 'there's something rather lovely about winter here – the light on the grey stone houses and cottages....'

'Would you call it *grey* exactly?' Beatrix said. 'Cotswold stone is said to be more honey-coloured, isn't it, though perhaps in a winter light....'

'And do you know,' Daphne went on, 'the iris stylosa are out in the garden. I always look out for them every year.'

'I expect there are some pretty gardens where you live now,' Beatrix ventured.

'Yes, people are great gardeners, but it's not the same, somehow. It's sort of...,' she hesitated, then said in a lower tone, '*suburban*, if you see what I mean.'

'But there's the common opposite your house, isn't there? All those dogs bounding....'

Daphne's expression softened and she smiled. 'Ah yes, the common. Bruce does so love the common – he has two or three walks a day. But of course here....' She seemed about to enumerate the advantages of village life for the dog, but Beatrix was quick to point out what a lot of traffic there was going through the village.

'I could take him in the woods,' Daphne said.

'But you'd have to keep him on a lead. Remember Sir Miles's game birds.'

'Yes, I'd forgotten that.'

'And then of course there's the problem of sheep and lambs.'

Beatrix persevered, trying gently to discourage Daphne from any idea that she might be happier living at the rectory again. The feeling she had experienced on seeing Daphne at the start of the evening had strengthened and now she knew that she was prepared to do all in her power to prevent Daphne from coming back to the rectory. Like a character in a Victorian novel, a kind of female villain, she might even take violent action, though she was uncertain as yet what form this could take. An idea had been germinating in her mind ever since Christmas, perhaps with the arrival of Graham's Christmas card and the possibility that Claudia might have chosen it for him, that it was more than ever her duty to 'do' something for Emma, since she seemed to be incapable of doing anything for herself. Having, as she saw it, failed with Graham (and had he really been worth the effort?), could she not do something to bring Emma and Tom together, unlikely though such a union might seem?

'I hear Miss Vereker paid a surprise visit,' Daphne was saying. 'I'd have liked to have met her, having heard so much about her. Tom said she was discovered wandering in the woods, somewhere near the site of the deserted medieval village.' She gave a little laugh. 'Of course that's all he thinks about, especially when he's by himself. I can't help wondering how he's been getting on without me. I suppose that's why I sometimes feel I ought to come back — for Tom's sake.'

'Oh, do you really?' said Isobel, coming back into the conversation. 'I think it's a great mistake to go back to a place. It would be like living your life backwards, wouldn't it? We must go *on* and *up*!' She gesticulated to that effect. She was evidently speaking in her role of headmistress, though her meaning was not altogether clear.

'But Tom has always been so helpless,' Daphne protested.

Beatrix produced a rather exaggerated laugh, as if to dismiss any idea of Tom being in need of any kind of help that Daphne might be able to give him. 'I shouldn't worry about your brother,' she said firmly. 'Men aren't nearly as helpless as women like to think,' she added, to strengthen her case. 'I think you'll find that Tom has....' She had been going to say 'other fish to fry', but rejected the culinary analogy as inappropriate, and substituted 'plans of his own.'

'Plans?' Daphne echoed in disbelief. 'Tom never has *plans*, except for medieval fields or villages. He hasn't said anything to me about any *plans*.'

'Beatrix thinks he may be thinking of marrying,' Isobel declared, bringing it out into the open.

'You don't mean he's asked *you* to marry him?' Daphne burst out in a way that could hardly be interpreted as flattering to Isobel.

Isobel flushed but said nothing, and again Beatrix wondered if she had entertained hopes of Tom for herself. On the other hand, perhaps she was beginning to realise what was in Beatrix's mind. The three women – Beatrix, Isobel and Daphne – stood in silence, looking over to where Tom was standing with Emma. They appeared to be laughing together over one of Dr G.'s antique surgical instruments.

Beatrix wondered how Emma was going to react to the plans that were about to be made for her. And, of course, how Tom would react, for that must also be taken into consideration. But he was less important and more easily manipulated, she felt – manipulation might not even be necessary.

As well as Dr G.'s antique surgical instruments, a few 'bygones' had been displayed on the table by which Tom and Emma were standing – examples of treen, such as a wooden apple-scoop and a dish and platter, and a collection of faded sepia photographs depicting groups of country people engaged in various rural activities that could apply to any region.

'Did your friend Dr Pettifer finish that book he was working on?' Tom asked. 'I was wondering whether we might ask him to give a talk to the society sometime.'

Emma hesitated for so long and seemed so doubtful that Tom feared that he might have said something 'out of turn' or dropped a brick in the way he knew the clergy sometimes did. Was the thought of Graham Pettifer still painful to her?

'I don't think he'd be likely to give a very suitable talk,' said Emma stiffly. She took up one of the sepia photographs and began to peer at it. 'People in front of the manor,' she said, 'on some nameless, long forgotten social occasion?'

'Oh then, perhaps you yourself,' Tom said, as if suddenly inspired, 'you've been in the village some time now and must have made notes on certain aspects of our life here, come to your own conclusions. You could relate your talk to things that happened in the past' — he indicated the photograph she was studying — 'or even speculate on the future — what *might* happen in the years to come.'

'Yes, I might do that,' Emma agreed, but without revealing which aspect she proposed to deal with. She remembered that her mother had said something about wanting to let the cottage to a former student, who was writing a novel and recovering from an unhappy love affair. But this was not going to happen, for Emma was going to stay in the village herself. *She* could write a novel and even, as she was beginning to realise, embark on a love affair which need not necessarily be an unhappy one.